That Winning Touch

D1652062

YO-EGZ-481

Other Avalon Books by Miriam Pace

WARM CREATURE COMFORTS

THAT WINNING TOUCH

Miriam Pace

AVALON BOOKS
THOMAS BOUREGY AND COMPANY, INC.
401 LAFAYETTE STREET
NEW YORK, NEW YORK 10003

© Copyright 1992 by Miriam Pace
Library of Congress Catalog Card Number: 92-71134
ISBN 0-8034-8931-5
All rights reserved.
All the characters in this book are fictitious,
and any resemblance to actual persons,
living or dead, is purely coincidental.

PRINTED IN THE UNITED STATES OF AMERICA
ON ACID-FREE PAPER
BY HADDON CRAFTSMEN, SCRANTON, PENNSYLVANIA

To Pat Kubis, who taught me so much, and to Vivian Doering, who got me started on the right path. Thank you.

Prologue

Elizabeth Stratton flashed her trainer ID to the guard and entered the stable area where the thoroughbreds waited for their races. Two stable hands sat chatting on upturned barrels. A large bay mare pranced nervously, her head arched, nostrils flaring. An anorexic-looking woman draped in fur and diamonds smiled proudly at the mare, indicating ownership.

"I like that one, Liz," Dennis Greer said, bearded face and narrowed eyes turned toward the bay mare. "Win, place, or show?" He consulted the race schedule in his hand.

"I don't bet the ponies, Dennis." A hot breeze swept Liz's red hair back from her tanned face.

Dennis laughed. "I've never known a trainer who didn't have a little action on the side."

A fat man smelling of booze and sweat jostled her, knocking the brim of her khaki campaign hat askew. She righted it with slim, muscular hands covered with calluses and scars. Beyond him another man, dressed in a flashy white suit, escorted a woman who giggled behind a slim hand.

A black mare, long and lean, with tight, well-trained muscles ridged with old scars, stood quietly amidst the

1

2 *That Winning Touch*

confusion, disdainful of the people and the other horses, her ears tilted forward alertly. Liz consulted the program. The mare was Ayala of Brentwood Farms. She quickly read through the statistics.

She pointed at the mare. "She has the look of a winner."

Dennis studied the animal, eyebrows lifted in a questioning arch. "She's a nag. Comes in dead last more often than not." He marked through the name with an X.

Liz grinned. What Dennis didn't know about horses could fill a very large book. Studying the mare's proudly sculpted head and long-limbed body, she decided she could use a mare like this. This could be the start of her dream. She left Dennis and headed for the paymaster's office. Ayala was entered in a claiming race—a field of horses that were for sale. Liz intended to buy her.

Once back in the clubhouse, Liz stood at the rail to watch the thoroughbreds file around the track to the starting gates, which were stretched across the dirt. She searched the crowd for Dennis and found him in his private box; the flashy-suited man was in the next one. Each horse entered the starting gate with skittish displeasure except for the mare named Ayala, who moved calmly, with a smug, superior attitude that announced she was a pro.

The alarm sounded, the gates opened, and the horses sprinted out, each one jockeying for a place on the field. Ayala kept back and let the others fight over the lead position. Then her jockey led her around the bunched knot at the rail, keeping her out of the crush. The first pole flashed, and the thundering herd of thoroughbreds careened into the backstretch.

That Winning Touch   3

Ayala stayed even with the leaders, her neck stretched taut, legs moving with intense concentration. Liz watched her through binoculars, mouth curved in an approving smile. That animal had breeding in her. Why was she in a claiming race? Anyone with the money could claim her, and a valuable animal would be lost—and Liz had just done that. The horse was hers. Silently, she urged Ayala to the front of the field and into the winning position.

As the field turned into the homestretch, Ayala slowed and dropped back. Dennis nudged Liz when she entered the box and sat down next to him. "Where have you been?"

"Paymaster's office. I put in a claim for Ayala."

The racing crowd went wild as the winner flashed across the finish line. Ayala came in dead last. Liz ignored Dennis's crow of triumph. Had she really seen what she thought? Had the jockey subtly pulled the mare back to keep her from winning? She felt a sense of great wrongness.

"Boy, did you make a mistake." Dennis flashed his winning ticket at her.

"I don't think so." Liz left the clubhouse for the stable area. Ayala stood off by herself. Her jockey was near her, his saddle in his hands, talking to Judd McLane, the trainer.

Judd was a small, wizened ex-jockey. He glared at Liz. "The word came down that you claimed Ayala. Mr. Brentwood's not going to like this. She's one of his favorites."

Liz shrugged. She didn't much care what Mr. Brentwood felt. "What went wrong?" she asked the jockey.

He shook his head, his eyes sliding away from her

direct gaze, his purple and gray silks rippling in the slight breeze. "She ain't got the heart no more."

"What do you mean, no spirit?" Liz demanded. "She's barely breathing hard. She should have won against that ragtag field of crippled rejects." Liz patted the sleek neck.

A stable hand led Ayala away. Judd and the jockey followed.

Dennis ran up to her, fanning a fistful of money. "A hundred and fifty bucks! You can't beat success."

Her eyes partially closed, Liz studied the departing Ayala carefully, from sweating withers to dust-caked nostrils. She was a seasoned veteran who had more breeding in her toes than most horses had in their whole body. She should have won a cheap claiming race, but didn't. Liz wanted to know why.

Chapter One

"I ASK you to reconsider, Miss Stratton." Chance Brentwood sat behind a large teak desk, scowling as he spoke. He tugged at his paisley tie, a muted gray that complemented the darker gray of his three-piece suit.

He had shiny black hair that seemed barely under control despite the cowlicks over each temple and the traitorous curls that fringed his ears. Liz wondered how much time he spent trying to look officious and pompous. Did he practice in front of a mirror? She had to admit the effect was intimidating, though wasted on her.

She sat quietly, her hands folded in her lap. She glanced at the edge of a high-heeled shoe, white damask edged in gold, that matched her creamy white suit. She'd dressed carefully for this interview, subduing her wild red hair in an old-fashioned chignon at the base of her neck and hiding her green eyes behind tinted glasses, hoping to mask their directness. Liz found the art of diplomacy a hard one to learn, since she had lived for so long with an outspoken, undiplomatic father.

She glanced around the office, a large, official-looking room with a row of diplomas on one wall and a bank of pictures showing Chance with a variety of Hollywood

6   *That Winning Touch*

beauties. He was a walking advertisement for his profession—entertainment law.

"The horse is mine," she said, bringing her attention back to the man in front of her.

Chance rubbed his chin with his fingers and glared. "I'm not only willing to buy the horse back but also to offer you double what you paid for her."

Her suspicions aroused, Liz stared out the window, pretending to reconsider her ownership of Ayala. Intuitively, she knew the horse was a winner. Something deep inside her said this animal was being misused.

"I'm sorry, but I like the horse. I don't see why you feel so passionately about an animal that isn't winning for you. After all, you allowed her to be entered into a claiming race to be bought by anyone with enough money." Liz waited for an answer, but Chance seemed to be thinking.

Finally, he said, "Since you won't sell Ayala back to me, we have nothing more to discuss."

"Yes, we do." Liz knew a lot more about Chance than he would ever know about her. She knew he was a man who liked to win. The irony of the situation was that his horses lost more often than they won. He bought, sold, and traded horses, trying to build a winning string, yet his animals continued to lose. Liz wondered why.

Chance sighed. "What's on your mind now, Miss Stratton?"

"You just fired Judd McLane." Liz swallowed a little nervously.

"He was incompetent."

Liz didn't agree. She knew Judd wasn't incompetent. "You've hired and fired five trainers in the last three years, Mr. Brentwood. They couldn't all be incompetent.

That Winning Touch   7

If you want your horse back, I'm willing to return her to you for the price I paid, if you'll hire me as your new trainer.''

Chance looked surprised. ''I'm afraid the answer is no.'' His eyes locked with hers, and she felt staked to her chair, a bolt of lightning pinning her down. ''You have no experience.''

Liz's lips narrowed. No experience. She'd grown up on the racetrack, following her father all over the Southwestern circuit and learning the business. ''My father was Giles Stratton,'' she said tightly. Anyone who had the barest knowledge of thoroughbred racing had heard of her father, who had trained three Kentucky Derby winners and won hundreds of races over his thirty-five-year career as a trainer.

Chance cleared his throat, looking a little uncomfortable. ''I know who your father is. If he were alive, I'd hire him in a minute. I can't take a chance with someone as inexperienced as you.''

Liz found herself standing, her anger rising. She knew horse racing backward, forward, and inside out. She'd grown up with straw in her hair, dodging kicking horses, getting up at four A.M. to exercise her dad's string, worming them, and shoeing them. She'd mucked stalls until the stench of manure was steeped in her skin. She'd slept on bales of hay pushed together to form a bed. She had more experience with thoroughbreds in her short twenty-six years than Chance would ever have in a hundred.

Gathering up her purse, Liz pushed away from the chair. ''Mr. Brentwood, why don't you pick up your phone and see how long it takes to get a new trainer? I guarantee you, not one reputable trainer will touch your

8   *That Winning Touch*

string. I'm staying at the Beverly Hills Hotel. I'm sure your secretary has the number.''

She remained composed until she closed the office door and stood in the long, quiet hall. Inside the office suite she heard the murmur of low voices. Abruptly, she stamped to the elevator. How dare he act as if she were nothing!

In the parking garage, she unlocked her RX–7. Like her father, she had a taste for sports cars and the funds to indulge herself. Her father had left her a tidy inheritance, and she intended to use it to build her own racing and breeding stable—starting with Chance Brentwood's Ayala.

She turned into the drive at the Beverly Hills Hotel and went directly to her secluded bungalow, set back from a path that bordered the Olympic-size pool. A lifeguard flexed overdeveloped muscles. A young woman in a skimpy leotard and tights served drinks from the bar. An aerobics class splashed in the shallow end.

Lounging around the pool, women in skimpy bikinis revealed large expanses of tanned skin and waved expertly manicured hands while they talked. Liz had never seen so many beautiful women before, from their José Eber coiffed heads to their brand-name sandaled feet. Hoping to catch the eye of anyone in the entertainment industry who might be casting, they seemed too calculated, too perfect.

So much flesh exposed to the searing sun made Liz wince. Her own fair skin burned red and raw without the sunblock she always kept handy in her purse and applied every morning.

In her bungalow, she draped her jacket over a chair. The short walk in the hot June sun had left her sweaty

That Winning Touch   9

and uncomfortable. Her skin itched. She kicked off her shoes, not caring where they landed, and unbuttoned her blouse as she walked into the bathroom and started the water in the huge Jacuzzi.

She returned to the bedroom to remove her skirt, hanging it neatly in the nearly empty closet. Liz traveled light. She'd learned to pack essentials and nothing more. Years of gypsy wandering had taught her to be well organized and precise in her needs. If she had no use for something, she didn't buy it. The only indulgence her father had allowed her had been books, hundreds of them packed into every crevice of their motor home.

After a long, luxurious soak in perfume-scented water enriched with bubbles and soap, Liz dressed in khaki pants and matching shirt. She walked out into the living room. Chance Brentwood was sitting comfortably in an easy chair, a soda in one hand and a cane lying at his feet.

"How did you get in here?" Liz would have to have a long talk with the management.

"Believe it or not, you left your door ajar." A boyish grin crossed his face, making him look younger and a little more vulnerable. "Considering the quality of the sharks inhabiting the pool area, I'd think you'd be more careful."

Liz shrugged. She'd grown up with sharks of every type—loan sharks, gambling sharks, and human sharks who haunted the racetracks searching for the elusive "big win." She took a soda out of the refrigerator. In the mirror behind the bar she saw Chance watching her with careful deliberation. Their eyes met, hers blazing with indignation and his wryly amused.

He looked away and color spread across his cheeks at

10 *That Winning Touch*

being caught ogling her. She forced her face to remain unsmiling as she sat down across from him and waited, knowing that he'd tell her the purpose of his visit when he was ready.

Outside, she heard splashing and laughter from the pool. A cool breeze filtered through the open windows. They were so close to the ocean, she could almost smell the salt. Liz loved the ocean. She'd surfed in Malibu during her four years of study at Pepperdine University.

Chance tapped his fingers on the arm of the chair. "I suppose you're wondering why I'm here."

"The thought occurred to me." Liz permitted a small smile. "I don't find strange men in my living room every day, especially men who have given me the impression my services are not wanted."

"I don't think 'services' is a good choice of words."

Liz chuckled, a rich, throaty sound that filled the room. "All right, then, work-related knowledge."

He stared at his soda can. When he looked up at Liz and smiled again, amusement lit his eyes, taking ten years off his age. She'd thought him middle-aged before, but realized he was probably no older than thirty-one or maybe thirty-two—too young to be acting like a stuffy old man.

"Is your offer still open?" he asked. "To take over the training of my horses, that is."

Liz pretended to think it over. In her mind, she'd already accepted, but she didn't want him to know that. "And what about Ayala?"

"She belongs to you. You took advantage of a situation I knew nothing about." He spread his hands across his knees. "Would you believe me if I told you I had no idea Ayala was being run in the claiming race? If I had

That Winning Touch 11

known, I would have stopped it. Ayala is too valuable to be treated in such a way.''

''Couldn't find a trainer to take over your stable, huh?'' Liz was rewarded with a deepening of the flush on his cheeks.

This man was no poker-faced lawyer. His emotions were revealed too easily. She wondered how successful he was as a lawyer, when the ability to negotiate depended so much on body language. Maybe his ability to empathize with his clients worked to his advantage.

''You've been talking to Dennis Greer,'' he said.

Liz wondered whether to reveal that she hadn't. Finally, she shook her head. ''I've talked to no one.''

He relaxed in the chair, twirling the can around and around. ''Please consider my offer, Miss Stratton. Liz, if I may. I've been a racing fanatic for years.''

She ached to accept his offer immediately, but she pretended nonchalance. Her future relations with him depended on her ability to keep control. Overanxious owners were big headaches to trainers.

Finally, she nodded. ''I accept.'' He smiled. ''But,'' she added, ''I expect you to keep your hands off and let me do the work.''

''Agreed.'' He struggled to his feet, grasping the cane to lean on. He held his hand out to Liz. ''I'll have my secretary draw up a contract.''

Liz shook his hand. ''I want a readable, understandable contract, and I'll phone her with the provisions.''

''Thank you, Liz.'' He limped toward the door.

She wondered what had left him with such a injury. She didn't ask. His problems were none of her business—just as hers were none of his.

12   *That Winning Touch*

He paused at the door, gazing back at her. Then he nodded as if she'd passed some sort of test and left.

Outside the door, Chance leaned on his cane and watched the women doing aerobics in the shallow end of the pool. Shaking his head, he called himself a fool. He'd come to find Liz Stratton to apologize for his rude behavior earlier and had ended up offering her the very job he'd refused to give her.

"Chance," came a high, lilting voice.

He turned to face a woman in a modest one-piece swimsuit with a towel draped over one shoulder and long brown hair pulled into a ponytail.

"Hello, Bunny," he said, offering his hand.

Ignoring his hand, she sailed up to him and kissed him on the cheek. Bunny Masters was slim and chic and pretty in an exotic, doe-eyed way. She was the product of everything that money could buy, and she'd once tried to buy Chance. He liked her and he'd even negotiated a movie contract for her, but she'd never made it in acting. She had dropped out to become a horse-racing groupie.

"I thought I recognized you ogling the bathing beauties." She tossed a tart look at the women in the pool.

"I do not ogle," Chance said with a wry grin. "Look maybe, but never ogle."

Bunny laughed, then said, "Where have you been keeping yourself? I thought you'd be at Hollywood Park last week when Ayala ran. She's your favorite. I heard she was bought by some trainer." Bunny looped her arm through his and walked with him toward the lobby.

With so many casually dressed men and women running around, Chance felt uncomfortable in his suit, and he was grateful to enter the muted interior of the hotel.

That Winning Touch

"I tried to buy Ayala back, but Miss Stratton wouldn't sell."

"You mean Liz Stratton?" Bunny gave him a wicked, knowing look.

"Yes, Liz Stratton. When she wouldn't sell Ayala back, I hired her to manage my stables." He still felt hollow anger. Ayala had been one of the best fillies born at Brentwood Farms. The mare had given him new hope, but her poor performance on the track had left him disappointed and dulled by horse racing. He felt as if he were throwing away good money, trying to keep his string of thoroughbreds going. For a moment, Liz had instilled new faith that he might yet achieve his desire, but cold reality now hit him. What could she do that the other trainers couldn't?

Brentwood Farms had once been the finest racing and breeding stable in California. Started by his grandfather in 1931, Brentwood Farms's horses had achieved fame and prominence in racing circles. The glory had faded a little under Chance's father's management, and now it seemed totally gone with Chance at the helm.

"Liz is a very good trainer, Chance. Trust her," Bunny said. "She has a sixth sense about horses."

"I wish I felt as confident about her as you do." Chance moved slowly through the lobby, using his cane to bolster the failing strength in his leg. He'd been in an automobile accident three years earlier, and pain had become a hated part of his life. "She's young and a little too brash for my own peace of mind."

"And you're so old? You're barely thirty. Give Liz a chance." Bunny playfully punched his arm. "She just might surprise you." She let go as Chance exited the front doors, signaling the valet for his car.

14 *That Winning Touch*

Chance waved at her as she bounced back inside. The valet brought his car, and he eased behind the driver's seat. As he drove back to his office down Wilshire Boulevard, he decided he could do worse than Liz Stratton. Dennis Greer had given her high marks. Chance would just have to wait and see.

Chapter Two

THE town of Del Mar boasted a racetrack built by Bing Crosby in the thirties. Its popularity was unequaled in the racing community, due to its location right on the ocean.

Liz loved Del Mar. She drove off the expressway, catching a glimpse of the racetrack and fairgrounds, now host to an annual fair. She saw the backstretch—the area of barns behind the track where the horses waited between races. The barns were empty now, but in a few weeks the racing season would start. She felt a thrill of excitement at the thought.

Long lines of cars waited to get into the parking area of the fairgrounds. She dodged the traffic, thankful she was traveling in the opposite direction, and continued inland toward the town of Rancho Santa Fe, the directions to Brentwood Farms on the seat next to her.

After a twisting ride on back roads, she turned onto a dirt road with a large, industrial-size mailbox. "Brentwood Farms" was printed on the side. The lane followed the perimeter of a low hill topped by eucalyptus trees. On the other side of the hill was a white, L-shaped house that opened in the rear onto a long covered veranda.

16 *That Winning Touch*

Behind the house were the barns. Curious horses poked their heads out over the half doors of their stalls.

A woman in a billowing apron approached as Liz opened the car door to a blast of hot air. ''I'm Margie, the housekeeper. Chance told me you'd be coming.'' She had a round, lively face and button-bright eyes filled with humor.

Liz had been apprised of the housing arrangement. Chance's household consisted of Margie, his niece, Andrea, and several hired hands. The hands lived in trailers on the other side of the barns, and Margie and Andrea lived in the house.

''I'm pleased to meet you.'' Liz opened the back of the Mazda, grabbing a suitcase by the handles.

''Let me take it.'' Margie grasped the handle and led the way into the house.

''Aren't my quarters near the barns?''

Margie shook her head. ''We have a small apartment at the very end of the house. Chance asked me to make it ready for you. The room is quite nice, with a direct entrance to the stable area so you don't have to go through the house. I know you horse people get up early.''

The house was cool and pleasant, with a living room decorated in earth tones and a collection of Navajo rugs on the floor. Liz followed Margie down a long hall past a cheerful yellow kitchen. Margie opened a door, and Liz found herself standing in a sitting room with a bar. Two sofas flanked a large flagstone fireplace and a door led into the bedroom.

''Chance said that you'll take your meals with the family. Actually, we all eat together—Allen Jaffe, Sam Cary, and occasionally Sam's son, Jack. Jack's a little

That Winning Touch 17

flashy, but he's okay.'' Margie walked into the bedroom and hefted the suitcase onto the bed.

The bedroom was more luxurious than anything Liz had ever lived in before, except for her overnight stay at the Beverly Hills Hotel, an expensive indulgence she'd probably never repeat. Margie stepped back and waited. Liz had never been very accomplished at small talk. ''It's very nice,'' was all she said as she mentally compared the elegance of the apartment to the tack rooms where she and her father had slept before he'd made enough money to buy a motor home.

The housekeeper beamed a huge smile. ''I knew you'd like this.'' She pointed at the French doors, which overlooked a pool and Jacuzzi. ''Your private entrance.'' She opened one door. A fly buzzed against the screen. ''Actually, all the bedrooms open on to the veranda. Chance designed the house. It faces the ocean and catches the breeze. Except for a few really hot days, we seldom have to turn on the air-conditioning.''

Margie started to unpack the suitcase. Liz tried to discourage her, but the housekeeper insisted. After receiving directions to the stable, Liz left her to the unpacking.

The pool was rectangular, a sparkling blue that shimmered in the heat and reflected the sun. A young girl about ten years old sat on a chaise, book in one hand, shaded by an umbrella. She glanced up as Liz skirted the pool.

''Hi,'' she said and jumped to her feet. ''I'm Andrea.''

''Nice to meet you.'' Liz studied the girl. She was obviously Chance's niece. The family resemblance showed in her clear blue eyes, smiling mouth, and curly, shoulder-length black hair.

''You must be Liz. Uncle Chance said you were com-

18 *That Winning Touch*

ing.'' She slid her feet into sneakers and bent over to tie them.

"I'm going out to the stables," Liz said. "Want to show me around?"

"Sure." Andrea looked delighted. She fell into step next to Liz, showing her the intricate gate locks and the path that led directly to the stables.

A man with hair that looked as if he had stuck his finger in a light socket wrestled a sack of feed from a flatbed truck. He paused and wiped perspiration from his forehead. "Miss Stratton?" he drawled.

"That's Sam Cary," Andrea said, a strange look on her face.

Sam walked in a stooped way that made him seem older than he was. He held out a gnarled, callused hand to Liz and she shook it. His fingers gripped hers, too tight for comfort. His grip tightened, and his lips disappeared as he sucked them in, waiting for her to respond.

"Are we having a contest?" Liz finally asked, her voice deceptively sweet, hiding the consternation she felt. She disliked having to prove herself over and over, and apparently Sam expected her to do so.

"Sorry." He wiped his hand on the seat of his jeans. "I guess you'd like to look around?"

"Andrea is showing me the barns." Liz smiled at Andrea, who hung back at a distance from Sam, her large eyes wary.

"Well, Andrea," Sam said in a patronizing tone, "you just go on back and sun yourself, or do whatever it is little ladies like you do. I'll take Miss Stratton around."

"Please call me Liz."

"Okay, Liz."

That Winning Touch 19

Andrea gave him a mutinous look and shook her head. "No."

"Now, Andrea," Sam said with a glance at Liz that told her how he loved kids, but couldn't be bothered to put up with their antics, "Liz is safe with me."

Seeing a fight brewing, Liz stepped between the two. "You're busy, Sam. I'll let Andrea give me the grand tour, and then I'll meet you back at the office and we'll talk."

Sam chewed his lip, his eyes darting back and forth from Andrea to Liz. Then he shrugged and went back to the truck.

Andrea grabbed Liz's hand and dragged her around a corner and out of Sam's sight. "Thanks," she said gratefully.

The stable complex consisted of three barns, each one designed to accommodate twenty horses. Most of the stalls were full. At the end a stallion poked his head out of his box stall and gazed at Liz curiously. He was gray with a rose undertone.

"That's Silverado," Andrea said proudly, stopping to rub the huge head. Silverado half closed his eyes in pleasure.

Chance wanted to breed thoroughbreds as well as race them. The horse, named for his peculiar silver color, had been born on the farm, the product of a mare descended from the great Nashua and a mediocre stallion, named SeeYaLater, whose bloodlines were better than his lackluster performance on the track. Liz understood why Chance had a lot of hope for Silverado. He wanted a premier breeding farm with Silverado at the helm.

Liz scratched the horse's sensitive chin. The large, sculpted head turned toward her. Then she walked down the feed alley to look at the mares. Most of Chance's twenty brood mares had spring foals with them, their sides already building with next year's crop. The long-legged foals gazed curiously at Liz, their velvet-soft noses turned expectantly toward her. Liz rubbed their chins.

Chance had twelve horses actively racing, all of them in one barn by themselves. The remainder of the stalls was given over to the horses of neighborhood children, rent-free in exchange for mucking out stalls and feeding.

A half-dozen yearlings had the south pasture to themselves. Liz gazed at the yearlings, studying them, already deciding which ones would be kept and which ones sold at the next auction.

Andrea trotted along with her, telling her the history of each horse.

"That's Attagirl," Andrea said, pointing at a handsome bay mare with a regal pose. "She won a couple of races in England before Uncle Chance bought her. He told me she neighs with a British accent, but she doesn't really." Andrea giggled, her affection for her uncle plain in her eyes. "He wants to breed her to Silverado someday, but Silverado hasn't performed too well at the track yet. Uncle Chance is awful disappointed in him."

"We'll see what we can do about changing his luck." Liz went from barn to barn, meeting not only Chance's horses but the neighborhood children's as well.

"Hey, Andrea." A boy ran up and gave Andrea a mock punch on the arm. He appeared to be about two years younger and two inches shorter than Andrea. "What ya doin'?"

Remembering her responsibilities, Andrea solemnly introduced Liz to her friend Pete Bernstein. "Hi!" He had an infectious, merry grin as he shook her hand.

That Winning Touch

"Hello, Pete." Liz found herself a little overwhelmed. She'd never gotten along well with kids when she was young. As an adult, she found them a little frightening.

"Did ya show her the rabbits?" Pete yanked Andrea's arm.

"Not yet."

"Rabbits?" Liz said.

"This way." Andrea ran toward the end of the last barn, where a huge awning shaded the side. Beneath the awning rows of cages held furry little rabbits. "This is Sir Lancealop. He's a French lop. You can tell because his ears hang down on either side of his face." Andrea opened the cage and ran her palm lovingly over the animal's back. "I'm showing him at the fair next week. Go on, pet him." She stood aside for Liz to put her hand in the cage.

"His fur is so soft." Liz was amazed at the silken texture. Her hand slipped around the long ears and she scratched. The rabbit's back legs jerked and she stepped back, startled.

"That's all right," Pete hastened to assure her. "He likes you scratching his ears."

Andrea closed the cage and moved on. She led Liz into an area with goats and sheep. "All my friends belong to 4-H. These are their current projects," she explained.

Liz nodded as if she knew what 4-H meant. "They look pretty impressive."

"Yeah," Pete said in agreement. He reached over a fence and petted a sheep. "This is my lamb."

"Doesn't look like a lamb to me." Liz eyed the large animal warily.

"A lamb is anything under a year old," Andrea explained.

22   *That Winning Touch*

Beyond the lambs were the cattle pens and then the pigs and hogs. Liz found out that 4-H was a club for kids who raised farm animals and then took them to the fair for competition and eventual auction. Andrea's rabbits were for show.

"I go to rabbit shows all over," Andrea said as they walked back to the house. "Margie takes me when Uncle Chance can't."

"Sounds interesting." Liz tried to picture the suave, urbane Chance Brentwood at a rabbit competition. The contradiction made her laugh.

"What's so funny?" Andrea asked.

"Nothing. Why don't your parents take you?" Liz knew she'd asked the wrong question from the clouded look that moved over the girl's face. "I shouldn't have asked. It's not my business."

"That's all right," Andrea said with an elaborate shrug of indifference. "My parents are divorced. Dad lives in Chicago and Mom's in Europe, just traveling around. She doesn't want me."

Liz knew how lonely a childhood could be without a mother. Her own mother, an exercise rider, had been thrown from her mount and trampled when Liz was five. Her father had never quite gotten over her death.

"I like living with Uncle Chance, anyway," Andrea said, looking a little happier. "He's my guardian. I love him the best."

Liz found herself wondering what kind of man Chance was when he wasn't being an officious lawyer. The thought of rich, unplumbed depths intrigued her.

Liz left the children and strolled into the farm office. There she found Sam, sitting in a rickety secretary's chair at the only desk in the room, his feet on the top as he

That Winning Touch

leaned back. "Finished your grand tour, huh?" He gave her a cynical look. "Let the younguns lead you around like you were—"

"Take your feet off my desk," Liz said softly. She had to assert her authority, as she felt that Sam had been at Brentwood Farms for years and expected a certain type of preferential treatment. Liz would give him the respect he deserved, but she expected him to recognize her position of authority, starting with the possession of her desk.

Sam looked startled. He stood up hastily, anger moving swiftly across his face and then disappearing.

The farm office was small and square with a tiny window that held a cracked piece of green glass. It was tucked into an area the size of a stall, and Liz guessed the office had once been just that. Two filing cabinets stood side by side on the far wall. Pictures of horses and voluptuous women decorated the wall. Liz reached up and removed the most offensive picture, folding it in half and dropping it in the wastebasket.

Sam watched her, his eyes narrowed, lips drawn into a straight, angry line.

A knock sounded on the door. A small, slim fellow about eighteen stood in the doorway. He barely weighed a hundred pounds, and before he even opened his mouth to introduce himself Liz guessed he wanted to be a jockey. His slim, slight body was almost perfect for racing and she could see the hunger in his eyes. She had once dreamed about being a jockey too, but gave it up when she topped out at five feet seven despite a short father and mother.

"Hi," he said. "I'm Allen Jaffe." He held out a square-shaped hand with a heavy ridge of calluses along the sides of the index fingers. "You must be Miss Stratton. Chance said you'd be arriving today." He gave her a disarming smile.

"Call me Liz. It's a pleasure to meet you," she responded. His hand was warm in hers, strong and firm.

Sam growled slightly under his breath and pushed himself to his feet. "I got to finish stacking the feed."

Allen stood aside to let Sam out the door. He half turned to watch him saunter across the feed alley to the storage barn.

"Sam's not happy about you being here," Allen said.

Liz had already figured that out. She didn't know what Sam's gripe was, but she figured Allen would tell her. She sat down at the desk, flipping idly through a stack of unpaid bills.

Allen turned back to her. "He thinks your job belongs to him, and he's mighty upset Chance didn't give it to him."

Liz nodded, feeling a little sorry for Sam, who reminded her of the men who hung around the backstretch broken by past dreams of glory. "I can understand his resentment."

Allen shook his head. "His resentment goes deeper than you think. Sam came to Brentwood Farms to manage the stables for Chance's father over thirty-five years ago. Sam was head groom for a Kentucky outfit that went bankrupt. He helped build this place."

Troubled at his revelations, Liz asked, "Why tell me all this?" She gave him a direct, no-nonsense look. She'd grown up with backstabbing gossip and betrayal on the backstretch. No one revealed such condemning information without a reason.

That Winning Touch 25

Color crept up his cheekbones. "I just wanted to warn you."

She let his remark pass. If Sam was a menace, she'd find out soon enough, even without Allen's warning. "Tell me what you do here." She smiled to let him know she wasn't upset but wouldn't tolerate further gossip.

"I exercise the horses." He grinned at her, his eyes alight with laughter. "I want to be a jockey."

She simply nodded. "I'll have to watch you awhile and see."

"Sam said he would put in my papers for me, if Chance made him trainer, but. . . ." Allen's voice tapered off at the sharp look from Liz. "Sorry," he mumbled.

"That's okay." Liz started out the door. "Why don't you take me on a tour of the horses and tell me about their habits, likes, and dislikes?"

"I thought Andrea already took you around."

"She did, but she didn't tell me much about the thoroughbreds."

Allen gave a short bark of laughter. "Andrea is a great tour guide, but she's more interested in her rabbits."

As they walked, he filled her in on the history of Brentwood Farms. "Chance's grandfather knew Bing Crosby and his partners were going to build a racetrack here at Del Mar. He bought up all the land he could in Rancho Santa Fe and Del Mar and somehow got into the business of racing himself."

Liz already knew this, but let him continue. By the time they approached the barn housing the thoroughbred racers, Allen had launched into a long talk about each horse's racing habits, preferred positions out of the starting gate, and favorite foods. She learned which ones liked carrots and which ones ate sugar cubes.

26 *That Winning Touch*

She and Allen spent the afternoon inspecting each horse. He told her the ones he thought would be ready for Del Mar, and the horses that should be held back and sent later to the Oak Tree Meet at Santa Anita after the Del Mar season ended.

Even though her opinions differed from his, Liz said nothing. She would make her own decisions on which horse went where. But until then, she let Allen rattle along, noticing that despite his lack of keen observations about the animals' conditioning, he loved them all and spent long minutes talking to each horse as if it were his very special child.

After Allen left, Liz made one more tour. She found Ayala's stall, her name engraved on a brass plate set in the lintel. Ayala would arrive tomorrow, ferried in a horse van from Santa Anita. Chance had given Liz permission to stable the mare in her old home. Once Ayala had rested for a brief bit, she had every intention of entering her at Del Mar. Then she'd see what type of breeding Ayala really had.

Chapter Three

CHANCE turned his Mercedes into the drive. He could see activity at the barns even though night darkened the sky. He hadn't intended to come home until Friday, but he'd remembered his promise to take Andrea to the fair. The Del Mar event was the second largest county fair in the state, and they never missed a year.

He parked his car between Jack Cary's pickup and a silver RX–7 that he'd never seen before. He assumed it belonged to Liz Stratton. The lights were on at the pool and he heard splashing and the cheerful laughter of children, Andrea's louder than the rest.

Chance had never quite figured out how he ended up being Andrea's guardian. Neither Chance's self-centered younger brother, Mitch, nor Mitch's social-climbing wife, Susanna, had ever shown the slightest interest in their daughter. He remembered the night Andrea was born. He had stood in front of the nursery window for an hour, staring at the tiny baby, unable to look away. Something in him, a yearning long dormant, had come alive.

Susanna had given her daughter a cursory, uninterested look, then gone to sleep. Mitch had never even come to the hospital, preferring to spend the night at Hollywood

27

28 *That Winning Touch*

Park betting thousands of dollars on horses that came in dead last. Chance had been angry at their lack of interest in their own child. And while they pursued their own interests, he had raised Andrea until Mitch and Susanna's divorce gave him sole custody of her.

The light in the stable office was on, a bright yellow square that illuminated the night. Chance used his cane to negotiate the treacherous flagstone path that led to the office. Inside, he saw Liz, head bent over a pile of papers, eating cookies as she read. The light bounced off her red hair, unruly tendrils escaping from her ponytail. She looked young and vulnerable and totally different from his first impression of her.

She looked up and suddenly smiled. ''Hello, Chance.'' She jumped to her feet and swept a pile of papers off a chair. ''Sit down. I was just going over the statistics for each of your horses. I'm trying to decide which ones to take to Del Mar and which ones to hold over until the Oak Tree Meet at Santa Anita.''

''Come to a decision?'' Chance asked, looking over her arm curiously.

''Yes and no.'' She handed him a sheet of paper, a computer readout. ''Deadly Justice is pretty good, but Prime Mover looks better.''

Chance looked at the sheet. He saw rows of figures and focused on them until he realized they were race results—wins and losses. The losses far outweighed the wins. Disappointment filled him.

''The stats don't look very good, do they?'' He handed the paper back to Liz.

''Afraid not.'' She frowned as she studied it. Then she opened a file folder and took out several more papers. Chance recognized the pedigree sheets of each horse.

That Winning Touch

"What are you planning to do?" he asked.

"Nothing, yet." She put the papers inside the folder and closed it. Then she slid the folder in a drawer. "I want to see the animals in action." She stood up and reached for a blue nylon jacket, which she tossed over her shoulders against the evening chill. "For the most part, you've been fortunate. You've had no major injuries in the last few years. All your animals are sound and in good health. I think I'll just wait a bit and see what develops."

She stood up and walked toward the door. Chance followed her out into the dark. Flipping off the light, she carefully closed the office door and locked it, pocketing the key.

"I'm going to walk around one more time." She turned toward the barns.

"I'm going inside. But I'd like to join you on your night rounds tomorrow."

She smiled and turned away. Chance headed toward the house. Night sounds filled the air around him. A cricket trilled, and a small animal rustled in the undergrowth. Chance could hear the horses moving restlessly in their boxes.

He passed the pool. The lights had been turned out and the children were gone. He opened the screeching iron gate, skirted the pool, and entered the house through the back door.

Margie stood in the kitchen. "Evening, Chance," she said as she stirred biscuit batter. "Dinner in thirty minutes."

Spicy, enticing aromas filled the kitchen. Margie was the best cook Chance had ever known. She'd worked for his mother for twenty years and he'd hired her out of

30 *That Winning Touch*

retirement to help with Andrea. Since her husband had just died, she'd been happy to accept his offer. Andrea needed her. Chance had done the best he could with his niece, but some things needed a woman's touch.

A puppy skidded across the kitchen floor. Chance stepped out of the way as Andrea ran in and flopped down on the floor. "Hi, Uncle Chance," she cried, jumping up again and throwing her arms around him. "You're early. You said Friday."

"Changed my mind." Chance hugged his niece. He loved the sweet, little-girl smell of her hair and the enchanting grin she gave him. "Where did you get the puppy?"

The reddish-brown puppy sniffed at Margie's ankles. Andrea scooped it up in her arms and kissed its pink nose. "Mama brought her." The puppy licked her face, and she giggled with delight.

"Keep her out of the kitchen," Margie ordered, stepping around Andrea.

"Do as Margie says," Chance said.

Andrea left and he turned to Margie. "When did Susanna arrive?"

"About an hour ago." Margie's dislike of Susanna Brentwood showed in her voice. She opened the refrigerator door and pulled out a package of carrots.

"I'd better go see her." Chance loosened his tie as he entered the hall. From the living room he heard the sound of high-pitched laughter, a short bark, and Andrea's voice.

He glanced in the living room. The Navajo rugs had been swept to one side to reveal the parquet floor. A fire burned brightly in the fireplace. Susanna lounged on a

That Winning Touch 31

sofa, her bright golden hair spread around her shoulders like sunbeams and her eyes dancing with laughter.

When she saw Chance, she tossed her hair back and grinned. "Hey, Chance. Come join the fun. Do you like the little gift I brought for Andrea?"

The puppy barked again and wiggled her curled tail. From the back of a recliner in the far corner of the room, Margie's eighteen-year-old calico cat viewed the activity with bored eyes.

Chance slipped off his jacket and draped it over the back of the sofa. "Nice-looking pup. Does she come with a pedigree?" He half expected Susanna to say the animal came from the pound. She seldom spent money on her daughter. Most of the time, Susanna couldn't be bothered to remember Andrea's name.

"One hundred percent Anatolian shepherd." Susanna smiled. "The breeder, a man I met in Mexico, will send the pedigree in the mail in a few days. Do you like her? Her name is Yildiz. That means something in Turkish, but I don't remember what."

"I've never heard of Anatolian shepherds." He gave the animal a critical view, seeing the long muzzle, floppy ears, and plumped tail, and trying to imagine the grown dog. The huge paws clued him that the pup would be big.

"I've got the brochure in my suitcase. I'll give it to you." Susanna said to Andrea, "Why don't you take the puppy outside now, dear?"

"Thanks, Mama." Andrea dutifully kissed her mother's cheek, then skipped from the room.

"I thought Andrea would like a pet," Susanna said. "Children should have responsibility, and pets are a good

32 *That Winning Touch*

way to teach that.'' She looked earnestly at Chance, as if begging him to agree.

He decided not to point out that Andrea already had a great deal of responsibility taking care of nearly fifty rabbits, assorted barn cats, and a horse. She already did an admirable job of being responsible.

''Are you staying?'' he asked.

''Heavens, no. What would I do here?'' Susanna leaned back in the chair, eyes narrowed as she watched Chance. ''I'll be leaving in the morning. Just a little visit to see my girl. Nothing special.''

Chance couldn't help but feel cynical. He saw Susanna so seldom, and usually only when she wanted something from him. The way she achieved her goal was to provide Andrea with inappropriate gifts. Although he had to admit the puppy looked like something Andrea would really enjoy instead of an unwanted toy.

''You needn't look so cynical, Chance.'' Susanna gave a tinkling, flirtatious laugh. ''I don't want anything for a change. Aren't you surprised?'' Her face took on a shuttered look and she averted her eyes, avoiding his questioning look.

In the distance, he heard a yowl of protest from the puppy, then Andrea came back into the room.

''Time to wash up for dinner,'' Susanna said in her best mothering voice.

Andrea glanced quizzically at Chance, who nodded in agreement. Susanna looked mildly irritated for a second, then her face smoothed and she smiled lovingly at her daughter.

''Go on, Andrea,'' Chance said in a mild voice. ''Dinner in a few minutes.''

That Winning Touch 33

"Margie made pot roast tonight," Andrea said as she left the room.

Susanna yawned. "How pedestrian. I can see you really enjoy the down-home life when you're not in Hollywood squiring about young, hopeful actresses."

She had been a young hopeful once. Chance had met her at a party given at a producer's house. He'd dated her twice before introducing her to his brother. She'd had several bit parts on television, but chucked it all away to marry Mitch Brentwood.

Chance had tried to warn Mitch that Susanna was a nice-enough person in her own way, but not wife material. Mitch had refused to listen, and Chance had seen his prediction come true when the marriage went bad and a divorce was granted. In truth he'd seen the immaturity in both of them—an immaturity that did not lessen even with Andrea's birth.

"I like being home," Chance said. "Excuse me, I'm going to change and wash up for dinner."

He left Susanna in the living room. She stared pensively into the fire, her face drawn into tight lines. Chance wondered what was really on her mind.

Liz was superstitious. She walked a circuit every night, checking on each horse, and she always started in the northeast corner of the barn layout.

She opened the doors and petted each horse, having already discovered the spots they liked best. Deadly Justice leaned into the webbing that crossed his door and nibbled at the carrots in Liz's pocket. She scratched his chin and he pushed against her.

Deadly Justice wasn't ready for Del Mar. He had a tendency to favor his right front hoof. Liz had felt a little

34   *That Winning Touch*

heat building in the hoof and ankle, and she wondered what had caused the injury. She would poultice it after dinner, having learned all her father's secret formulas for drawing heat out of sore legs.

Next to Deadly Justice's stall, Prime Mover dozed, leaning against the wall. He looked fit, and Liz smiled at him as she rested her elbows on the bottom half of the door.

"They look good, don't they?" Sam said as he joined her, leaning over the half door.

"Yes, they do." Prime Mover's ears twitched. Liz closed and latched the stall door.

"They all have their own personalities," he said.

"I find horses endlessly fascinating," she replied as they moved down the feed alley toward the next row of stalls. A gray barn cat moved sinuously through a small hole cut in the bottom of the door to Silverado's box. Liz opened the door, and Silverado eyed her as he nibbled at the cat's tail.

"That's Swallow," Sam said, pointing at the cat. "He and Silverado are pals."

Horses had a tendency to form attachments with other animals. Liz had known them to like goats, sheep, and dogs, but she'd never known one to attach himself to a cat.

Swallow meowed, jumped on a ledge just under Silverado's nose, and curled up into a ball, his tail covering his nose. Silverado nosed at the cat, then turned toward Sam and Liz. She held out an apple to him. He sniffed the apple and took it, juice dribbling down his chin as he chewed.

Sam closed the door. They checked the other horses,

That Winning Touch   35

then stood out in the dark night, the smell of fresh-mown hay surrounding them.

"I love these horses like they were my own," Sam said. "Chance and I watched Silverado being born. We have a lot of hope for him."

"He's an impressive colt."

"I've been here thirty-five years." Sam stared out over the valley spread before them like an inverted cup. The last heat of the day had disappeared. Night breezes brought a chill, vaporous fog from the ocean.

"You've got a lot of time invested in this farm."

"I raised my boy, Jack, here. He and Chance used to be good friends when they was kids." Sam drew spirals in the dirt with the toe of his boot. "I got dreams."

"So do I, Sam."

He drifted away, his shoulders hunched, his hat pulled forward over his eyes. Liz heard a sheep bleat over in the area she called the 4-H annex. From near the house, a puppy barked, a sharp yipping sound.

Liz turned toward the house, skirting the pool, steam rising as warm air mixed with the cooler ocean air.

"Nice night." Chance stood at one end of the pool, staring down into the water. He joined her.

She slowed to accommodate his halting steps. She wondered what had disabled him in the prime of his life. She felt a touch of pity. Yet she couldn't help but be aware of him as a man.

He stopped and turned toward the barn area. "I grew up with racing in my blood."

"Me too." She smiled at him, barely able to make out his form in the darkness. Yet she felt as if she could reach out and touch his warmth. "I grew up on the backstretch

36 *That Winning Touch*

and know practically every track between Mexico and Seattle.''

''You've had quite an unusual life.''

''I always thought it was perfectly normal. Three or four different schools every year. It's remarkable I ever learned anything.'' She remembered her father taking her out, moving, and enrolling her in the next school, showing her birth certificate to prove her age. The kids in her new class would always start teasing her because she upset the established pecking order. But when they learned she lived at the racetrack, their teasing usually turned to curiosity, then awed respect.

Margie opened the kitchen door and poked her head out. ''Dinner's on the table.''

''Shall we eat?'' Chance offered her his arm.

Her fingers brushed his skin and an electric shock jolted her. ''Let me wash up and I'll be right there,'' she replied, keeping her voice steady, trying to ignore her response to him.

She decided long ago never to become involved with the men she worked for or with. Liaisons among the racing folk never seemed to work out. The gypsy wandering did not promote a normal family life. Liz knew her goals were incompatible with marriage. No man wanted a wife on the racing circuit, racing other peoples' horses, traveling ten months out of the year. She would simply have to do without marriage.

In her room, Liz washed quickly, combed her hair, and changed to clean jeans and shirt. She ran out the door, rounded a corner, and bumped into a tall, slim man. Beyond him, she had the impression of a room with a desk and bookshelves, but he closed the door before she could see more.

That Winning Touch   37

"You must be Liz Stratton," he said in a hearty bass voice. "I'm Jack Cary, Sam's son." He looked about twenty-five, with sleek black hair and pale blue eyes. "Just cleaning up for dinner." He led the way to the dining room.

Chance sat at the head of the table, with Margie on his right and Andrea on his left. Sam and Jack sat down next to Margie. Chance indicated to Liz to sit at the foot.

"We don't stand on formality," he said. "Just dig in."

The aroma of fresh-baked biscuits filled the air. A spiral of steam rose from a bowl mounded high with chunks of potatoes and carrots. Sliced meat lay on a platter.

Liz started to reach for the biscuits when she became aware of a woman standing at her elbow. The woman was very attractive in a petulant sort of way.

"You're sitting in my place," she said to Liz.

"Susanna," Chance said, "no one has any specific place to sit. I suggest you get your food before it disappears." She sat down abruptly in the free space.

Sam heaped his plate with the food and added three biscuits, which he liberally buttered. Jack took a more modest helping. Susanna took only a small sampling of each dish and then pushed the food around her plate with her fork.

Liz felt a chill dampen the spirits at the table. Susanna had the look of a woman who had an indulged life. She wore designer clothes and sported a hairstyle that for all its simplicity obviously came from an expensive salon.

Susanna said in a high, artificial voice to Liz, "You're the new trainer. Chance didn't tell me you were a woman."

Chance then introduced her to Susanna. Liz was sur-

38 *That Winning Touch*

prised that she was Andrea's mother. With her ultraslim figure and youthful face, she barely looked twenty-five.

"It's a pleasure to meet you," Susanna gushed, though she looked far from pleased.

Liz piled food on her plate and dug in, eating as she tried to understand the undercurrents of tension that rippled around the table. Chance looked angry. Andrea was unusually quiet, cutting her carrots into minute pieces and then pushing them away. Only Sam seemed immune. He focused on his food, chewing methodically as if nothing in the world were as important as what he ate.

"Eat your carrots, Andrea," Susanna ordered in a motherly voice.

"I'm eating, Mama." Andrea's face looked mutinous.

Margie smiled in approval at Liz's generous helpings. She was hungry. Her day had started long before dawn and would not end until she'd checked all the animals one last time.

"I envy a woman who can eat and eat and eat and never gain an ounce," Susanna said with a tiny giggle.

"We should take Liz to the fair, Uncle Chance," Andrea said. "Then she could eat her way from one end to the other."

"And what about me?" Susanna asked.

Andrea gave her mother a long look. "You're leaving tomorrow morning."

Susanna blushed, a rosy-cheeked flush that made her look like a sixteen-year-old girl.

"I've been to the Los Angeles County Fair," Liz said. "I should think all county fairs are alike."

Andrea grinned at her. "Del Mar is better. Please come. Uncle Chance, ask Liz to come."

That Winning Touch   39

Chance looked at Liz, a question in his eyes. "Why not come along? You'll like Del Mar."

"I need to think about it."

"Go, why don't you?" Susanna interrupted rudely. "Andrea won't let you rest until you give in."

Liz smiled at Andrea. "I think it sounds like a lot of fun. I'd be delighted."

Andrea clapped her hands. Susanna looked petulant.

"Sam says the horses look good." Chance spooned pan drippings over an open biscuit. "He thinks they'll all be ready for Del Mar."

"Not all of them," Liz replied. "Deadly Justice is favoring his right front hoof and I felt heat in it earlier, and Summer Storm isn't eating."

Sam waved his hand in the air. "Deadly Justice will be fine. I'll ice the ankle before I go home. Summer Storm is fickle. He starves one day and gorges the next."

"I don't think Deadly Justice's injury is that simple." Thoroughbreds were bred for speed, not hardiness. The smallest injury could upset the delicate balance of their health. Liz never left any injury untreated. After dinner, she'd go to the vet supply for the ingredients in her father's poultice.

Sam's voice rose belligerently. "I've been around horses all my life. I know a simple bruise when I see one."

"Sam," Chance said, his word like a warning shot across the bow of a ship, "I hired Liz for her expert knowledge. She's not questioning your experience, she's safeguarding the horses in her charge."

"Are you saying I don't have experience and expert knowledge?" Sam pushed his plate away, his face set into stubborn lines.

40   *That Winning Touch*

"I'm saying that Liz knows what she's doing in her capacity as trainer," Chance said, a touch of anger in his voice.

"And I don't." Sam clamped his lips tight shut and glared at Liz, then Chance.

"Pop," Jack said, "Liz is good at what she does too."

"And me," Sam grumbled, "I'm just a stable grunt who doesn't know left from right."

"Sam," Chance said softly, "you're the best wrangler in California. You have the knowledge to breed the right horses and get prize-winning foals from them. Liz knows how to make them win." His tone said no further objections would be tolerated.

Sam subsided, but darted angry looks at Liz. She stirred uncomfortably in her seat, her appetite gone.

Susanna followed the exchange avidly, trading glances with Jack. Liz became more uncomfortable. She stood up, pushing her chair back. "Excuse me." She left, preferring the company of the horses.

Chance followed her. "I apologize for Sam's behavior. He expected to be put in charge of the stables."

Outside, stars twinkled in the dark sky. A cooling breeze flowed over the valley. She headed toward the barns, slowing her steps so Chance could keep up.

"Sam's been here more than thirty-five years. He felt he deserved the trainer position."

"You don't have to explain." Liz flipped on the light to her office and was immediately touched by the feeling that something wasn't right.

"Is something wrong?" Chance asked.

"I don't think so." But she could see that the papers on her desk had been rearranged and a pile of files that had been straight before was slightly askew. Deciding

That Winning Touch 41

that her imagination was working overtime, she smiled. "Everything is still strange. Sam will get used to me. I won't challenge his authority with the brood mares. I think he fears he'll be left out somehow."

"Maybe." Chance's face was unreadable. If he had any thoughts on the matter, he kept them to himself. "I want to take a look at Deadly Justice's sore hoof. That's been happening a lot lately."

"It has?" Liz straightened the files on her desk and glanced at the rearranged papers. The top paper was a listing of the statistics on Silverado. Liz specifically remembered filing this particular piece of paper in Silverado's folder. How had it gotten out? Who had removed it, and why?

"Judd mentioned Deadly Justice's sore hoof too."

"Sore hooves could mean trouble." Liz headed toward the door, turning out the light as she exited. "I'm going to make a poultice and apply it to Deadly Justice's ankle." She headed toward her car, her keys jingling.

Later that night, after Liz had applied the poultice to Deadly Justice's ankle, she sat in her bedroom in the dark, staring at the barns, wondering what was going on at Brentwood Stables. When she'd had her fill of brooding, she pulled her bathing suit out of a drawer and decided she'd swim for a while. Maybe exercise would help clear her head.

Chance, out for a late swim, watched Liz slice the water cleanly with barely a splash. She stroked across the pool and back again. She was a strong swimmer with elements of professional training in her style.

He sat down at the edge of the pool, dangling his legs in the warm water and enjoying the therapeutic relief of tense muscles. His leg hurt tonight, and he stared at it, dismayed by the ridged scars and deep crevices that scored the musculature. He thought of the horrified responses he usually received when other people first viewed it. How would Liz react? It seemed important to him.

The underwater lights lit her body as she moved swiftly from one end to the other. After a half-dozen laps, she swam to him, drew herself up on the side of the pool, and reached for her towel. Curls of mist rose from the pool.

"So, what happened?" she asked, startling him. "To your leg." She toweled her hair dry with casual nonchalance.

"I was in a car accident," Chance said. He wondered if he should tell her the whole story. How Mitch had been driving and arguing vehemently with Susanna, not paying attention to what he was doing. Chance often wondered if the guilt of the accident had been the underlying reason why Susanna and Mitch had been so willing to turn Andrea over to him.

"It must have been some accident." Liz kicked at the water.

He waited for her revulsion, but nothing came. Playfully, she splashed him. He splashed her back. Suddenly, she shoved him into the water.

Chance grabbed her hand and she fell in with him, her body warm against his. She streaked past him, slicing cleanly through the water, and Chance chased after her. He laughed out loud and she joined him. For several minutes they swam, then Chance felt exhaustion overtake him. He sat on the steps in the shallow end, breathing hard.

That Winning Touch   43

"You're out of shape." Liz joined him on the step.

"You're not." He admired her strong arms and muscular shoulders.

"I like to swim."

"As much as you like horses?" The teasing tone in his own voice surprised him. He couldn't remember ever teasing a woman before.

"Horses are my life," Liz said soberly. "I can't even visualize a life without them." She gazed across the pool, her eyes distant, as if she were looking at long-buried memories.

Chance felt an overwhelming desire to kiss her. He stopped himself, afraid of frightening her. For all her tough exterior she seemed vulnerable.

"My father gave me my first pony when I was two years old," Chance said. "By the time I was eight he had me exercising the thoroughbreds."

Liz nodded in agreement. "I grew up in the backstretch of every racetrack in California. My father followed the circuit—Del Mar, Pomona, Santa Anita, Hollywood Park, and then back to Santa Anita. I miss him so much." She sounded lost and alone.

Chance remembered her father, a big man with a shock of wiry red hair that seemed to stand up from his head. "How did he die?"

"Heart attack, one day at the track. He wouldn't listen to his doctor's advice. He was only fifty-two." Her voice trembled. "I never got to say good-bye."

"Isn't that always the way it is?" Chance found himself holding her. The water gently lapped against them. He turned her head toward him and kissed her.

Liz stared at him for a moment, then she rose, water

That Winning Touch

cascading down her body. Without another word she left him, rushing across the patio toward her apartment.

Not until the door closed behind her did Chance move. He pulled himself painfully from the pool and tossed his terry-cloth robe about his shoulders. He picked up her towel, folded it neatly, and left it hanging over the back of a patio chair. She'd find it in the morning. Then he limped into the house and his own bed to dream about Liz and the sweetness of her reluctant kiss.

Chapter Four

EARLY-MORNING dew sparkled on the grass. The sun, a pale yellow ball low in the eastern sky, barely lit the horizon. Wispy fingers of fog hung over the low hills. The air smelled of fresh manure and newly cut hay.

Liz had spent several days working out schedules and getting to know the horses. Now she stood outside the exercise area, a stopwatch in hand, preparing to analyze each horse's performance before deciding which animals would race at Del Mar and which wouldn't.

With one foot resting on the bottom rail, she nodded at Allen. He rode Silverado, cantering the huge iron-gray horse around the track. A cloud of dry, throat-clogging dust rose at each step.

At her nod, he urged the horse into a gallop. At the first pole, horse and rider flew across the dirt. Liz clicked the watch in her hand. At the second pole, she stopped the watch and waved at Allen, who pulled Silverado out of the hard gallop, slowed him to a canter, a trot, and a walk.

"How was it?" Allen asked after he had walked Silverado around the track and back to Liz. The big horse pranced, looking back at the track as if he wanted to take

46   *That Winning Touch*

another try at it. He breathed easily, tossing his head, and reached out to nibble playfully at Liz's hand.

"Good time at the quarter pole," Liz said with a smile. "Walk him tomorrow and go for an easy workout Tuesday."

Allen patted the horse's glossy neck. "Have you decided which horses you'll be taking to Del Mar?"

"I've tentatively chosen Prime Mover, Betsy Ross, and Silverado," she said, knowing everyone's curiosity.

"Betsy Ross!" Sam said. He spat a stream of tobacco juice at the grass. "That mare's going on six years old. She can't compete anymore and should be retired to brood mare."

"I disagree. There's more power in her than you know," Liz said with an irritated glance at the brown-stained grass. Sam had a lot of habits that annoyed her. Smoking and chewing tobacco, especially around the stables, were two of them.

"I was against Chance buying her. She's past her prime. But Judd McLane insisted on her. He said she had a lot of life left in her." Still glaring, Sam turned away from Liz to his son, who approached mounted on a brown pony. His face softened briefly as he watched.

Jack reined in the pony to join the conversation. He wore a smartly styled Stetson, and the gold links of his necklace jingled with the rhythm of the horse. Jack sat the pony uneasily. When he rode, he bounced too much in the saddle, showing no understanding of the movements of a horse. Yet he wanted to help exercise them, and he displayed thorough knowledge of each animal's habits.

He gave Liz a long, appraising look that set her teeth

That Winning Touch 47

on edge. He winked. She ignored him and turned back to Sam.

"You think Betsy Ross would be a better brood mare than a racehorse?" Liz wondered what Sam had based his observation on.

"That's what I think." Sam spat again, the stream of juice narrowly missing the shiny brown toe of Liz's boot.

She didn't draw her foot back. Her silence dared him to spit again. He backed away from the unspoken challenge.

"She doesn't look burned out." Liz thought the mare still had the competitive edge that made a good racehorse. Retiring her to brood mare would be premature as long as she had no serious injuries and appeared capable of winning.

"I hate to say it, Pop, but Betsy Ross looks like she's got some life left in her." Eager to sow seeds of dissension, Jack jumped into the conversation. "Why not run her a while longer?" His eyes seemed to warn Sam. Sam shrugged.

"You don't know what you're talking about," Allen said to Jack with a disgusted snort. Silverado moved restlessly, sensitive to the hostility flaring between the Carys and Liz.

"I do too." Jack's smirk intensified. He eyed Liz insolently, his gaze traveling up and down her body.

Liz ignored the sly, ogling look. Jack was a nuisance, but one she could manage. She'd met his kind before, the "get-rich-quick" hopefuls who hung around the tracks and tried to be big shots with the owners. His look turned petulant at her casual dismissal.

"Cool the animals down and put them away," Liz said

48 *That Winning Touch*

with a glance at her watch. Every horse had been exercised. Allen would oversee their cooling down.

Sam walked away, leading Betsy Ross. Jack dismounted and walked with him.

"Liz—" Allen began. He leaned forward over Silverado's neck, his eyes shifting between her and the Carys.

She didn't like Sam or Jack. They thought they could wear her down by insinuations, drive her away with their insulting familiarities. They didn't know her. She was her father's daughter, with a stubborn streak a mile long and twice as wide.

"Ignore them." Liz tilted her head at the departing men. "I've met that type before."

"But you don't know what they did to Judd. . . ." Allen stopped. He looked guiltily at the ground.

"Since you've started, you might as well tell me." Liz took the reins under Silverado's chin and tugged him toward the barn. Judd McLane was a good trainer. She had thought that Chance had fired Judd because he'd entered Ayala in the claiming race. Allen's words told her differently. She wanted to know why, not because of worry over what Sam might do but because any stain on Judd's reputation had the potential to ruin other trainers and supply ammunition to organizations that considered racing sinful.

Silverado followed her willingly. Despite a tendency toward nervous pacing, he had a nice, even-tempered personality. But would he run when he needed to prove himself? His last two races had been erratic, uneven messes. He'd come in first in one, and last in the second. She chewed at the thought briefly until Allen's next words brought her back.

That Winning Touch   49

"They told Chance that Judd was taking kickbacks from suppliers." Allen looked unhappy.

"And he wasn't?" Liz frowned. Of course he wasn't. Judd McLane was one of the most honest men she had ever known. Even her father had admired his integrity. "Did you tell Chance about your suspicions?"

"No." Allen ran his hands down Silverado's shiny neck, entangling his fingers in the horse's mane. "Who would listen to me, a runt kid only eighteen years old and wanting to be something better than Jack Cary?"

"*I'm* listening to you." Liz thought Chance would too. He struck her as being a fair man.

"I liked the old man," Allen said angrily. "I know everyone considered him burned-out and all, but Judd was nice to me. Chance wanted to help him, and Judd planned to help me get my apprentice jockey papers, and. . . ."

"Don't worry about it," Liz said reassuringly. "Sam won't try his little tricks on me. I'm not Judd." But he *would* try something. His little defeat at the dinner table the other night had not set well with Sam. Though he treated Liz with civil respect, his attitude was tinged with anger.

"But you can't—"

"I said, don't worry about it." Liz glanced at her watch again. She had just enough time to shower and change for the fair.

Andrea and Chance had insisted she come. Andrea had told Liz she *had* to see the 4-H projects and visit the exhibition halls. At the edge of the barn area, she could see Andrea with her rabbits, feeding them and taking the time to hold and pet each one. A goat followed her, sniffing at the heels of her shoes.

50 *That Winning Touch*

"Have a nice time today," Allen said hesitantly.

"I will, thank you." She grinned at him. "I've never seen Del Mar outside racing season. Today should be fun."

In the few days she'd been at Brentwood Farms, she'd learned that Allen was a responsible, conscientious young man who would make a good jockey. He had an intuitive feel for horses that Sam lacked, no matter how much he protested or proclaimed the benefits of his thirty-five years of experience.

After showering, she stood in the window of her bedroom and looked up at the overcast sky, wondering if the day would be hot or remain cool. Finally, she chose dark-blue cotton pants and a peach silk blouse with the sleeves rolled up to her elbows. She found a comfortable pair of canvas loafers. As she walked out the door, she grabbed a wide-brimmed straw hat.

"You look nice," Chance said when Liz walked into the living room. "And you're on time. I've never known a woman to be on time before."

"You said you wanted to leave at nine-thirty." Liz believed in being punctual.

"I like women who are on time. Now if only Andrea. . . ."

The girl walked into the living room dressed in bright red shorts and a shirt with a silk-screened unicorn on the front. She'd twisted her long blond hair into a ponytail and tied a scarf around it, the ends swinging along with her hair. Margie followed.

"Are you sure you don't want to come, Margie?" Chance asked.

"Not today. I've got too much to do." She laughed, a high musical trill. "You have a nice time and watch

That Winning Touch
51

out for those sharp hawkers in the exhibition halls. They'll have you believing you can't live a rich, fulfilled life without their very special product to enhance it." Margie tugged playfully at Andrea's ponytail.

"I'm ready." Andrea stood next to Chance as if waiting for his approval.

"You look pretty good." He admired her with a warm smile. "I've never been so lucky before—two beautiful women with me on the same day." He kissed his niece on the cheek.

Liz smiled, seeing a lovely ten-year-old girl trying to act grown-up, yet looking exactly what she was—a ten-year-old girl. She remembered being ten, desperate to outgrow the awkwardness of the age and be treated seriously. She wanted to tell Andrea to enjoy her childhood, but the girl would have no more understanding of Liz's intent than Liz herself had had when her father tried to tell her the same thing.

Andrea gave her uncle one of her beautiful and too-rare smiles. Her eyes sparkled and glowed with anticipation.

"Ready? Jack is bringing the car around." Chance picked up a baseball hat and settled it on his head. His eyes flicked appreciatively from Liz to his niece.

"Jack isn't coming, is he?" Andrea said, an anxious pull to her lips.

"No, he's just bringing the car around," Chance assured her.

Andrea's anxiety disappeared and she smiled again. The doorbell rang and she ran to answer it, returning with Pete in tow.

"Hi!" Pete had been thoroughly scrubbed, looking quite different from the grubby little boy Liz had met the first day. His hair had been neatly tamed and his freckles were free of dust. "Jack left the car running."

"Then let's go." Chance herded everyone toward the door.

A beige Mercedes sat on the drive, its motor purring. Chance held the car door open for Liz and ushered Pete and Andrea into the back. Liz slid inside, appreciating the plush upholstery and luxurious interior. But as much as she liked the Mercedes, she much preferred her RX–7.

"Relax. Today's a play day," Chance said to her when the ranch had been left behind in a cloud of dust.

"I was comparing your car to mine," she admitted.

"And you prefer yours." He chuckled and glanced over at her, his eyes sparkling.

Sitting next to him left Liz feeling peculiarly breathless. Chance was slipping under the guards she'd erected to keep her life simple and uninvolved. It made her uneasy to think she could so easily fall into the vulnerable position of being in love. She hadn't liked the helpless feeling the first time around, the inability to control the situation, to keep a man at a distance. And Chance was not the kind of man who stayed at a distance.

He parked in the fairgrounds' lot and paid the entrance fee. Beyond the gate, the fair was already crowded, with parents shepherding broods of children. Solitary adults strolled along, peering into merchants' stalls, and lovers walked hand-in-hand, oblivious to the chaos surrounding them.

Chance pointed at an information booth. "If you get lost, we'll meet here," he told Andrea and Pete. He took Liz's hand. His fingers curled around hers and she shivered. A current of raw energy seemed to flow from his

That Winning Touch 53

hand to hers. She tried to pull away, but he tightened his grip.

"I hope you like to eat," he said, using his cane to navigate through the crowd. "The food's expensive, but a lot of it is quite good. This is a great day for noshing."

"Noshing?" Liz asked uncertainly.

Chance looked at her in surprise. "Trying a little bit of everything. Haven't you ever gone noshing on Fairfax Avenue in Los Angeles? They have some of the best deli counters and little specialty shops in the city. You go into each one and sample some of the food, then go on to the next one." At the blank look in her eyes, Chance shook his head. "Liz, you've had a deprived childhood. Today I'm going to show you the fine art of noshing. We'll start down at the end at a little booth with the best deep-fried zucchini in the world."

He took her arm and led her to the right. Andrea and Pete ran ahead toward the animal barns, where Liz could hear the lowing of cattle and the bleating of goats and sheep.

"I'm bringing my lambs here first thing tomorrow morning." Pete explained to Liz that he had to stay all week to tend his animals and do barn duty. "Mom and Dad have a camper in the backstretch. Mom does barn duty too. Dad goes to work."

"It sounds exciting," Liz said, not really certain she understood what he was saying. In the barns, she saw kids in white 4-H uniforms with green scarves around their necks and green hats on their heads. Looking closely at the felt hats, she saw stars and badges sewn along the sides. The kids groomed their animals or fed them. A couple of girls stood behind an information booth and

54   *That Winning Touch*

answered questions. Two boys about Pete's age waved at him.

"That's Jimmy Morris and his brother," Pete said. "Jimmy has his veal calf here. He told me yesterday that he sold it at auction Friday and made four hundred dollars. I want a veal calf next year. Is that all right, Mr. Brentwood?"

"You know the rules, Pete." Chance examined a veal calf in a stall with a For Sale sign tacked up on the overhead brace.

"You can buy the animals?" Liz saw several other For Sale signs over the heads of other tethered veal calves.

"Yeah," Pete answered, and then he was gone, running down the alley to join a group of boys already clustered around Andrea.

"We've been deserted." Liz laughed.

Chance straightened, leaning heavily on his cane.

"Don't worry about them." He took her hand again and led her down the alley. He examined several other veal calves.

"I suppose you buy your meat for the whole year here," she said.

"As a matter of fact, I do," he said. "Where else am I going to get USDA prime on the hoof? For a lot of these kids, this is a business."

"I can see that."

"These aren't pets," Chance said, petting a handsome young steer with a Sold sign tacked to a beam over its head.

Liz was extremely conscious of Chance's hand around hers. His fingers moved briefly up and down her palm in a light caress. She felt chilled even though the day was hot. She found him staring intently at her, watching her

That Winning Touch 55

with a look that made her ill at ease. She shrugged out of his grip.

The next barn sheltered goats and hogs. In between the second and third barns was a fenced area surrounded by bleachers. Parents watched while 4-H members paraded around a ring with their goats on leads. Two judges stood in the center.

Beyond the goat and hog barns were the sheep barns. A small building off to one side housed poultry and fowl. Liz wandered down the long rows of cages, looking at capons, pigeons, and breeds of chickens she didn't know existed. On each cage, cards gave information about the animals.

Andrea came running up. ''This is the rabbit barn,'' she said to Liz. ''Tomorrow night, these animals will be gone and the cages set up for rabbits. The judging starts on Thursday morning. I had a Best of Show last year.''

''I suppose there's more than one breed of rabbit.'' Liz's experience was limited to the wild jackrabbit variety and Andrea's fancy lops.

''You'll see,'' Andrea said enthusiastically. ''Uncle Chance, can Pete and I stay here for a while? We'll meet you back at the information booth.''

''At one-thirty,'' Chance said.

''Thanks.'' Andrea ran off to join a group of white-uniformed girls. They all giggled, walking off arm-in-arm with a couple of older boys watching them.

''Why don't we go back the other way?'' Chance suggested. ''The flower-and-garden exhibit is interesting.''

''I'd like to see the exhibition halls,'' Liz said. Margie's words about the interesting products were still in her mind.

''We'll visit them too,'' he promised. Several young

girls pushed between them. Liz stopped, confused for a moment, then Chance took her hand again and led her out of the barn and down a path running along one side of the building.

Outside, men hawked balloons advertising the fair. Booths held rows of stuffed animals and other curiosities. One exhibit held a Jacuzzi with a young woman sitting inside showing off a nubile figure encased in a very skimpy bikini. Her forty megawatt smile enticed the men but slid over the women.

They walked back past the entrance gates and into a covered exhibition hall filled with the fragrance of flowers. "Do you like flowers?" Chance stopped at an exhibit of bonsai, admiring the tiny Oriental plants trained into such unusual, delicate shapes.

"I don't know." When Liz thought of flowers, she saw hothouse roses and carnations encircling the neck of a race-winning horse.

"You're in for a treat." He guided her into the exhibition hall, where exotic arrangements from local nurseries enticed them.

Again, she tried to shrug his hand away from her arm, too aware of the rushing emotions in her, but he held on tightly. Chance Brentwood disturbed her.

After they saw the orchids and other exotic floral displays, they went on to the exhibition halls where hawkers sold their merchandise and professional hucksters showed unusual articles guaranteed to make life easier for anyone lucky enough to own them. Liz had no idea what she would do with such items, though she admired the expertise and the sales pitches.

At one booth, she stopped to watch a pretty young woman with a smooth delivery demonstrate a chopping

That Winning Touch 57

knife that did one hundred and one things. But Liz knew she would chop her fingers off if she ever tried to use it. She told Chance what she was thinking. He threw his head back and laughed, his face alight with enjoyment.

"Your fingers are too pretty to be chopped off by a knife." He raised her fingers to his lips and kissed them lightly.

A blaze of emotion ran through Liz. Her fingers tingled with the warmth of his kisses. And it felt so natural to wander along the aisles with him next to her. She stopped to admire a rug woven in South America with stylized Inca designs along the borders.

"Margie would like that," Chance said musingly.

"If you buy it now, you'll have to carry it all day," Liz pointed out in a practical tone.

"I'll rent a locker." He signaled a small, fat man with dark hair slicked back from a round, shiny forehead. "How much?"

Liz wandered over to a row of water dispensers while he bargained with the man.

"Have you ever tried our purified water?" a salesman asked. He was young, with wavy brown hair and vibrant blue eyes. He poured water into a tiny cup and handed it to Liz. "Take some of our literature. Our water is the best in California."

Liz sipped it, aware that she was thirsty.

"As an introductory offer, we'll give you one free five-gallon bottle of water with your purchase of three bottles," he continued with the practiced ease of a salesman who understood his audience. He flirted with her, making her feel as though she were the most important person in his life—at this moment.

A laugh bubbled in Liz's throat. "Thank you, but I

58　　*That Winning Touch*

don't think so.'' She felt a little guilty sampling his water while refusing his offer. She felt Chance behind her. He held the rug under his arm. She smiled and he grinned. They walked away and another interested woman took Liz's place at the dispenser.

"Let's head back to the gate. The kids should be waiting for us," Chance said. "I'll find a locker, and then we'll eat."

Finding Andrea and Pete was easy. They were sitting under a palm tree and spotted Liz before she saw them.

"Where's Uncle Chance?" Andrea asked.

"Renting a locker." Liz led the way back to the lockers and saw Chance talking with a woman who smiled up at him with an intimate familiarity that made Liz pause. The woman left him, walking quickly away without a backward glance.

"Shall we eat lunch?" Chance took Liz's hand in his and started down the main thoroughfare, which was lined on both sides with trailers. Each trailer was a delight of pleasing aromas: fried chicken, hamburgers, candied fruits, and corn on a stick.

"Where do we start?" Liz asked, bewildered by the variety.

"How about here? We'll work our way down to the carnival zone and then sample some of the rides."

"Uncle Chance," Andrea cried, pointing at a deep-fried hot dog on a stick, "I want a corn dog, please."

"Want one, Liz?" Chance asked.

"No, thanks," Liz said. Beyond the corn-dog trailer was another trailer advertising chicken wings. "I like chicken wings, though."

He nodded and handed money to Andrea. Then they purchased chicken wings with barbecue sauce. They

That Winning Touch   59

strolled along the thoroughfare, being pleasantly jostled by other people who ate and gawked.

Chance insisted on trying a spiraled, deep-fried bread with powdered sugar on it. Liz found the pastry too sweet for her. They shared a slice of indifferent pepperoni pizza. She licked tomato sauce from her fingers.

"There's so much to choose from," she complained, wanting to take samples from every trailer. She felt as if she wouldn't eat again for two weeks. She'd had fried zucchini, pineapple on a stick, fish and chips, and a half-dozen other delicacies, some excellent, some the worst food she had ever eaten. And yet she enjoyed every bite.

"Why don't we sit down and let Andrea and Pete explore the Fun Zone? I'm not much for rides that go upside down anyway." He indicated a group of picnic tables set up in front of a stage. On the stage, a little girl about five years old tap-danced around a huge stuffed dog, singing, "How Much is That Doggy in the Window?".

"Yes, let's sit down," Liz agreed with relief. The heavy eating had made her drowsy. The sun had long since burned off the overhead haze, burning down on the fairgrounds with unrelenting intensity. Not even a cool ocean breeze stirred the air.

"How about a beer?" Chance suggested.

"Just a soda, please."

He returned with two sodas and a small wedge of cheesecake. He offered Liz a bite, but she shook her head, knowing she'd never be able to swallow. She wondered how he managed to stay slim and muscular when he liked to eat so much. Just the thought of another bite of food made her slightly nauseous. Being so close to Chance also did little for her nerves. He smelled like a man who'd

60 *That Winning Touch*

been working long and hard in the sun—a raw, musky scent that reminded her of day's end at the racetrack.

"Enjoying yourself?" He finished the cheesecake.

"Oh, yes." She watched the little girl on the stage drag the stuffed dog after her as she left. Her place was taken by several older girls who did a delightfully sweet hula despite its amateur look. "I don't think I could eat another bite of food. I'm glad this happens only once a year."

He grinned. "You know, you're quite different when you're away from your horses."

"Am I?" She didn't feel any different. She didn't tell him that his horses were never very far from her mind. Racing was ingrained in her.

"Yes, you are. And I like that person." He smiled warmly at her, his fingers curling around her wrist.

A shiver traveled along her spine at the sight of that smile. Her heart thumped painfully in her chest. Her pulse leaped wildly under the amused look in his green eyes.

"In fact, I wouldn't even mind kissing that person," he said, leaning forward, his lips so close he almost touched hers.

Liz felt his warm breath fan across her cheek. She jumped back, her eyes wide with alarm. For one wild moment, she'd wanted to kiss him with the same longing. She'd wanted to feel his lips on hers, his breath mingling with hers.

In an undertone, he said softly, "I'll claim that kiss before the day is over."

The hula routine was replaced by a woman who launched into an enthusiastic rendition of "Some Enchanted Evening" from *South Pacific*. The lunch area became crowded. A young woman with two children

That Winning Touch 61

asked Liz if she could share the table. Liz nodded absently, not really listening. She felt Chance's body heat through her clothes. Yet she was cold.

He watched the stage. A country-and-western singer sat down on a stool, his guitar across his knees as he adjusted the microphone. He delivered lukewarm jokes, claimed a friendship with an international star, and launched into a performance no better than the hula dancers or the girl with her stuffed dog.

Liz swallowed nervously, thinking about Chance's promised kiss. She could still feel his earlier attempt, his fingers stroking her chin, his lips just barely missing hers. No other man had roused such turmoil in her, such confusion. She wondered why. She examined her emotions inside and out, wondering if she dared trust herself. She'd committed herself to her profession. Did she want the complication of love in her life? Her father had taught her to be independent, to reach for her goals, her dreams. Marriage had never been in her dreams. Besides, she'd already tried love and it had been a disaster.

"Let's see if we can track down the kids." Chance got up heavily from the table, stumbled, and caught himself. He looked tired, and there was a gray cast to his skin that alarmed her.

"Maybe we should think about heading home?" She glanced at her watch and discovered it was nearly five. Where had all the hours gone?

Andrea and Pete returned. Liz announced her desire to return to Brentwood Farms, and was relieved when Chance readily agreed.

Neither child protested. They had done all they'd wanted. Andrea held Chance's hand, looking as tired as he. Under one arm she clutched a stuffed bear, won in

62 That Winning Touch

a carnival game booth. Pete licked a cherry Popsicle that melted faster than he could eat, the syrup running down his fingers.

Liz had not gotten the chance to go into the second exhibition hall, nor into the art building. Though she had a mild interest in photography and art, she preferred to go home. When Chance stood up and leaned on his cane, she knew his strength had come to an end. She could visit the fair another day.

The drive home was quiet. Liz yawned, fighting her weariness. She rubbed absently at a sore spot on her heel.

Pete and Andrea, with the recuperative powers of the young, sat in the back of the car comparing prizes won at the carnival games. Their voices were low and unobtrusive. Andrea giggled.

Liz leaned her head against the headrest, closing her eyes, aware of Chance's strong hands on the steering wheel, his eyes on the road, and his tall, powerful body so close to her. She bit at the inside of her mouth. For the first time in her life, she felt a vague dissatisfaction with herself. From her earliest memory, she'd always known she would work with thoroughbreds. She'd never questioned her determination. But now, sitting so still and quiet next to Chance, she wondered about her life, about her decisions. She wondered if she'd made the right choices.

"Your nose is burned." Chance turned onto the road leading back to Brentwood Farms. The car followed the twists and turns of the narrow two-lane road. But instead of turning onto the lane leading to the house, he continued onward, following the road that climbed up into the brown hills. Looking back over her shoulder, Liz could see the haze of heat blanketing the valley below.

That Winning Touch 63

She rubbed her nose, the skin tender to the touch. "I enjoyed myself. Thank you." She wasn't a person who played hard; her enjoyments were few and far between. She wondered if she'd become too serious, too zealous in the pursuit of her life, in the avoidance of love.

"The fair's a once-a-year indulgence." Chance touched her cheek, then returned to driving.

He skirted the base of a hill and turned onto a driveway that climbed straight up. At the top stood one of the most beautiful homes Liz had ever seen. Situated on an outcropping, the house overlooked the valley. Far below, Liz saw Brentwood Farms. In the distance she fancied she could see the diamond-tipped waves of the Pacific Ocean.

A woman in a brief jonquil-yellow bathing suit came out to the driveway and waved at the car. Her pale-brown hair curled about narrow shoulders. She smiled, her eyes crinkling up at the corners. She was exquisitely beautiful, with that petite form Liz often envied but was not programmed in her genes.

Pete lowered the window and yelled, "Hi, Mom! Boy, did we have a great time!" He squirmed with excitement.

Chance brought the car to a stop. Pete's mom approached and leaned over to look inside.

"You all look tired," she said. "Care for a cold drink before heading back?" She smiled and put her hand on Chance's arm.

"No, thank you, Marian," Chance replied. "Liz Stratton, this is Marian Bernstein, Pete's mother."

"Hi." Marian patted Chance's arm with a beautifully manicured hand.

Liz gave an answering smile. She looked down at her

64   *That Winning Touch*

own hands, large and square, the nails blunt cut across the tips—working hands for a working woman.

A little girl ran toward the car. Pete jumped out of the car, scooped the toddler up in his arms, and hugged her.

"Thanks for taking Pete." Marian backed away from the car.

Chance waved, put the Mercedes in reverse, backed up to the garage, and turned around. They drove back to Brentwood Farms.

After the day of noshing, Liz didn't think she was hungry until she sat down at the dinner table with Andrea and found herself devouring fruit salad and a ham sandwich. Margie beamed appreciatively at them, but frowned at the empty chair at the head of the table.

"Uncle Chance had to make some phone calls," Andrea said in between mouthfuls of sandwich.

Liz only nodded. Margie did not look appeased. She disappeared into the kitchen and returned moments later with a tray. She carefully made up a plate and then went into the hall to deliver the tray to Chance's office.

"Do you like Uncle Chance?" Andrea said, helping herself to a second sandwich.

"What a question to ask," Liz replied in a cool tone, implying a dislike of her curiosity.

"You don't have to frown at me. I saw you holding hands at the fair," Andrea said with a sweet smile. "I don't like him when he's busy. He never has time for me. He's always in Los Angeles."

"He took you to the fair today," Liz pointed out.

"I want to do more things with him."

"But he *does* love you." Liz looked thoughtfully at Andrea, seeing an insecure young girl in need of a little

That Winning Touch 65

attention. She wondered why Chance had custody of Andrea and not her own mother.

Andrea cupped her chin in her hand. "If he loves me so much, why won't he let me stay in Los Angeles with him instead of keeping me here? He says it's because the schools are better here than in Los Angeles."

The more Andrea talked, the more Liz began to think she was really talking about something else. Her mother, perhaps? Her father? "You have to be somewhere," Liz said. "Why not here? Be thankful he didn't send you to boarding school."

"Is that what your dad did?"

"Yes." Liz remembered the pain of her first year away from her father. She'd been fourteen, unhappy and insecure. Always the odd one out, she'd understood the animals in the science lab better than the girls in the dorm. Not until she made the swim team did she receive any level of acceptance.

"Did you worry that your dad didn't love you?" Andrea asked.

"No, I never doubted my father's love." She'd always known how he'd treasured her, his only child. "He loved me as much as your uncle loves you."

"My mother doesn't love me." Andrea rose from the table, grabbed a sandwich, and walked to the door.

"You might tell your uncle how you feel," Liz suggested. "He can explain why he's made the decisions most affecting you."

Andrea shrugged and ran out. Liz let her go without further comment, though her own appetite had disappeared. She left half a sandwich and most of her fruit salad on her plate, and wandered out of the kitchen toward the barns.

66   *That Winning Touch*

"You'll get your nice clothes dirty, Liz," Allen said.

She leaned against the open Dutch door of Silverado's box stall and shrugged. The horse nuzzled her hand with his soft lips. She gave him a carrot she'd taken from the kitchen.

"Enjoy yourself today?" Allen stood next to her, dwarfed by her tall frame. He stroked Silverado's silken nose.

"I had fun," she answered. She patted Silverado's neck and scratched behind his ears. "Thanks for staying all day today and watching the horses."

"My pleasure. Got to go. See you tomorrow." He wandered away. After a few minutes, Liz heard the sound of his motorcycle. She closed the door of the stall and went back to the house, satisfied that everything was quiet in the barns.

Her room felt lonely. She turned on the television and sat down on the sofa to watch it, but fell asleep instead. When she woke, the room was nearly dark. Stiffly, she rose, stretched, and was pulling on her bathing suit before her mind had even made a conscious decision.

The water was beautifully still in the night air. Liz had the pool to herself. She parted the water cleanly and swam quickly to the other end. She loved swimming, the feel of the water against her skin, the coolness. When she finally grew tired, she drew herself up on the side. Chance was sitting in a lounge chair watching her.

"You've been at that for nearly half an hour. After all the walking you did today, I should think you'd be exhausted."

"I took an impromptu nap," she said with a laugh. "I woke up so cramped, I thought a little exercise would

That Winning Touch

help.'' She rolled her head on her neck and moved her shoulders back and forth to loosen the tight muscles.

She pulled her towel about her. He stood up and limped to where she sat on the edge of the pool and sat down next to her, dangling his legs in the water.

His nearness disturbed her, unleashing a confusion of feelings.

''I liked being with you,'' he said, kicking splashes of water toward the middle of the pool.

''I had a fun time too.'' Liz struggled to feel at ease with him. His warmth radiated over her.

''Never one to commit yourself, are you?'' He ran a finger up her arm.

She shivered at his touch, staring at his hand as it moved over her skin to rub at the ache between her shoulder blades as though he understood exactly where she hurt. Then his finger traced a line up her neck to her chin, her lips, and her cheek.

He's going to collect his kiss, she thought. His face bent close to hers. His lips touched her cheek, her chin, and the line of her lips, nibbling at her skin, bringing a dusky blush to her face. She tried to move her head, but he held her chin firmly with his fingers and forced her to face him.

''You're not going to run away tonight.'' His voice had a sweetly tender quality to it.

Liz leaned toward him. Her pulses raced. Her heart pounded loudly in her ears. She prepared to abandon herself totally to the kiss, yet a part of her held back, afraid, unwilling to take the chance, to reveal her soul.

The next thing she knew, they were floundering in the water. Grabbing the edge of pool, Chance laughed so loudly he swallowed water and coughed heavily.

68   *That Winning Touch*

"What happened?" Liz asked in confusion. She found her footing on the bottom of the pool.

"I think we fell in." Grabbing her, he pulled her through the water toward him and wrapped his arms around her.

Liz clung to him, staring at him wide-eyed. The warm water swirled around them. He kissed her, his warm lips on her cool ones, his body pressed against her chilled skin.

With a gasp, she broke away. Chance went under. By the time he surfaced, Liz stood on the edge of the pool.

He hooked his elbows over the edge of the pool. "Don't run away. I won't hurt you."

She shrugged into her robe and tied the belt savagely tight about her waist.

"Liz," he said, no pleading in his voice, only a sincere gentleness.

She paused, undecided. A tingling radiated through her. She wanted to stay, to feel his arms around her, but fear returned. She fled back to her room, locking the door behind her, half afraid Chance would follow.

At the window, she peeked at him from behind the anonymity of the curtain. He dragged himself out of the pool and reached for his cane to lever himself to his feet. Then he briskly toweled himself dry and walked toward the house.

Long after he had left the pool, Liz stayed pressed to the wall, tears dripping down her cheeks. When she recovered, she showered and went to bed, the sheets feeling damp and uncomfortable. She tossed restlessly and slept badly, dreams of Chance superimposed over a faceless thing that pursued her, haunted her. She yearned for

That Winning Touch 69

something elusive that seemed to hang just beyond her reach. But when she reached for it, the feeling dissolved.

Liz lay staring at the shadowed ceiling, feeling as if something monumental should have happened to her, that her life should have changed in some way. But the turn was not taken because she had been afraid.

Chance stalked into the house from the pool, his exhaustion forgotten under the dismay of rejection. He walked down the hall swinging his cane like a weapon. A light shone in the living room. He entered, walked to the bar, made himself a martini, and had the cocktail halfway to his lips before he remembered his decision never to drink again. He poured the martini down the sink and stood staring at the drain.

"Problems, Chance?" Margie sat in her favorite armchair, half hidden by a floor lamp. Her feet rested on a stool: a book lay open in her lap. She wore a robe with pink mules on her feet. On a table sat a glass of wine. "Do you want to talk about it?"

He poured himself a club soda, added a lime slice, and went to sit across from her. "Liz is the most exasperating woman. Every time I try to get close to her, she skitters away like a nervous foal. I thought today would be different. She seemed to be at ease with me, and then. . . ." He slammed his drink down on the table, then mopped up the spill with a napkin. "Sorry," he muttered.

Margie snapped her book shut and set it on the table. "You're dealing with a woman who isn't sure what she wants. I suspect she's been hurt before. Badly."

Chance paused, trying to analyze his thoughts. Even as Margie verbalized her concerns, he knew he'd already been thinking the same thing. "I'm glad to know it's not

70   *That Winning Touch*

me.'' He drank the club soda while new thoughts turned
over in his mind. "Not my leg." Anyone committed to
him would have to accept the fact that he was maimed.

"You don't believe that." Margie took a sip of her
wine. "You've had half the Hollywood starlets chasing
you at one time or another, before *and* after your accident.
Liz strikes me as someone who doesn't judge a person
by appearance.''

Chance flipped aside a corner of his robe to stare at
his leg. He often thought he should have let the doctors
amputate it as they first wanted to. He wouldn't be carrying around this scarred reminder for the rest of his life.
He had refused the amputation. He preferred the leg in
any condition to a plastic-and-wood prosthesis.

"I really like Liz," he said.

Margie laughed. "Liz is a nice woman. I like her too.
Try being more patient.''

"Andrea likes her too," Chance said.

"Andrea is desperate for motherly attention. Susanna
loves her, but not the way Andrea needs. And Susanna's
love isn't quite as generous as it should be.'' Margie
gazed into the fireplace, her face thoughtful.

Chance didn't add that Susanna was much too selfish
and self-centered to be interested in her own daughter,
whom she viewed as a rival. And then there was Mitch.
Chance worried constantly about his brother. Not even
at Andrea's birth had Mitch showed any interest. Both
parents, for reasons of their own, had given up all claims
to the girl. They'd drifted in and out of her life, showing
up with inappropriate gifts and then disappearing again
for months at a time. Chance knew that Andrea felt abandoned by them and occasionally by him, because he
worked in Los Angeles and kept her here at the farm.

That Winning Touch　　　71

Margie took another sip of her wine. "It's getting time for me to go back into retirement, Chance. I'm not young anymore. You did promise me a little cottage somewhere around here. I don't want to be too far away."

"You'll have your cottage, I promise." Margie had given up a lot to help him with Andrea. He'd always be grateful to her for stepping in to care for his niece after the messy divorce. He owed her so much.

Margie picked up her book and her wine, and hoisted herself out of the chair. "While you're paying attention to Liz, try paying some extra attention to Andrea. She needs you."

He looked at her in surprise.

"Andrea feels that you don't love her," Margie went on.

"But I do, very much."

Margie sighed softly. "She's insecure, Chance. When was the last time you told her you loved her? She's only a child whose own parents don't bother to see her. She's starting to feel that no one loves her." She said good night and left Chance to his thoughts.

He sat in the chair. The automatic timer on the light switched off, leaving him in darkness. For a long time he sat wondering how he could show Andrea his love, but Liz kept intruding on his thoughts. Finally, he went to bed. No solution occurred to him in his dreams, and he woke the next morning feeling very much at a loss.

Chapter Five

At four o'clock in the morning, Liz rose, dressed, and attended the horses during their workouts. The thoroughbreds returned to their stalls by ten o'clock—exercised, fed, and groomed. She spent the afternoon working. Like any business, thoroughbred racing consisted of more paperwork than action.

After the evening feedings, she fell into bed exhausted. She didn't return to the pool for a late-night swim.

She didn't trust herself, not after her emotions had betrayed her. She remembered the first and only time she'd ever been in love. His name had been Timmy Allanby, and he'd hurt her. She remembered him as clearly as if she'd seen him an hour ago.

Timmy had been a groom working for her father and she'd just graduated from Pepperdine. Her experiences with men had been limited. And Timmy was exciting, handsome, and charming.

They had shared a love of thoroughbreds, and Liz thought that he was perfect, only to find out that Timmy had feet of clay. Then a scandal involving illegal drug use and a sweepstakes-winning thoroughbred barred Timmy from ever working in racing again. He said he'd done it for money. But Liz realized they had basic ethical

That Winning Touch   73

differences that would never be reconciled. They had said good-bye, and she'd nursed a hurt that still seemed to fester despite four years of distance.

Because of Timmy, she'd vowed to concentrate on her profession. It was a vow she'd kept until the night before, when Chance's nearness had filled her with an urgency that left her breathless. She didn't want to love again, to be hurt again. Yet each moment with Chance brought her inexorably closer to the pain-filled reminder of what love had once been for her.

"I told you he didn't love me!" Andrea screamed as she slammed the kitchen door, interrupting Liz's early-morning coffee break with Margie. "I told you." Tears streamed down Andrea's cheeks, anger and hurt darkening her blue eyes. She stood in front of Liz accusingly.

"What's wrong?" Liz asked calmly, gently.

"He's gone. He went back to Los Angeles. And today is the day I have to take my rabbits to the fair." She spat each word. Her hands clenched and unclenched.

Margie said softly, "He left early this morning while you were at the exercise track. He said important business had come up. He talked to Sam before he left."

Liz turned back to Andrea. "I'm certain your uncle has a good reason for leaving." A wave of disappointment mingled with relief swept over Liz. She touched Andrea's shoulder. The girl jumped back, glaring, and wiped her eyes with the back of her hand.

"He forgot." Andrea fought to control herself. "Sam won't take me. He says Uncle Chance gave him too much work to do. But he's just sitting in your office with his feet on your desk and smoking. Uncle Chance doesn't

74   *That Winning Touch*

like Sam smoking around the horses. Jack said he'd take me, but I'd rather kiss a skunk.''

"What time do your animals have to be there?" Liz glanced at the clock over the sink. Ten minutes after ten.

"By noon." A hopeful expression shone in her eyes.

"Then let's get them loaded up. I'll take you." Liz drained the last of her coffee in a gulp and turned to Margie. "Where are the keys to the truck?"

Margie pointed wordlessly at the ring of keys hanging next to the door. Liz took the one labeled *truck*. She opened the kitchen door. Andrea ran after her.

"I'll bring the pickup around to your cages," Liz said, heading for the garage. Andrea loped off toward the back of the storage barns, her blond hair swinging wildly back and forth.

The garage was open. The truck was parked on the far side next to Liz's Mazda. An empty space separated the beige Mercedes from the RX–7.

Jack strolled into the garage. He wore skin-tight jeans and a plaid shirt open to the waist. Gold chains blinked in the sunlight.

"I told Andrea I'd take her," he said. He leaned against the truck door, watching Liz, arrogance in his eyes.

"I'll do it." She pushed him out of the way and opened the door to the pickup. She was dismayed to discover it was not an automatic shift. *You've become spoiled, girl*, she thought ruefully, trying to remember back to her father's old Oldsmobile and its stick shift. She'd been sixteen and he'd tried to teach her how to drive it, but she'd never gotten the hang of it. The car either died or bucked like a bronco.

"Think you can drive it?" Jack jeered.

"I drove trucks like this before you were born." Liz's

That Winning Touch 75

statement wasn't true. She didn't learn to drive until she was fourteen. By her clock Jack would have been an obnoxious twelve-year-old at the time.

She climbed into the cab, started the engine, found reverse, and slowly backed out of the garage. Her foot slipped off the clutch, the truck darted backward, and Jack jumped out of the way. He tossed her a superior look. "Call me if you need an expert." He sauntered away.

"When pigs fly," Liz said between clenched teeth. She started the truck again, eased the clutch up, and backed out smoothly. Turning down the lane that ran by the side of the barns, she nosed the truck alongside the annex.

Andrea had packed the animals into wire traveling cages, three to a compartment. Liz stopped the truck, got out, secured the cages in the bed of the truck, and locked the tailgate.

"Let's go," she said.

Andrea climbed into the cab next to Liz, her face still rigid with the lingering anger she harbored against her uncle.

"He always does this," she complained, pounding her fist into her knee. "He forgets." She rubbed fiercely at her eyes.

"For the moment, can we just table this discussion? I need directions." Liz felt bad for Andrea, especially since she felt Chance's abrupt departure was her fault.

"Turn right," Andrea said at the road.

Liz followed Andrea's directions until they found a road she recognized. Confusion reigned on the streets surrounding the fairgrounds. Cars streamed in unbroken

76   *That Winning Touch*

lines into the parking lot. Over thirty thousand guests per day visited the fair, creating traffic snarls and gridlocks.

Liz approached an entrance barricaded with wood saw-horses painted white with red stripes.

"Go around the barricade." Andrea sat on the edge of the seat, her seat belt looped loosely around her. She tugged nervously at her hair. "Park there." She pointed at a line of cars on either side of a double-doored entrance into a barn. "What time is it now?" She bit a thumbnail.

"Eleven-thirty." Liz slid the truck into a parking spot. People walked in and out, carrying cages of rabbits or wheeling them inside on wagons.

"I forgot the wagon." Andrea hopped out of the cab and strode anxiously back toward the tailgate.

"Then we'll carry them in by hand." Infected with Andrea's anxiety, Liz knew Chance would never desert his niece. He must have said something to someone. Sam, perhaps.

"Hi, Mrs. Temple," Andrea called to a woman standing at the door. "Mrs. Temple's my project leader," she told Liz.

Mrs. Temple gave her a frazzled smile. "You're here."

"Sorry. This is Liz Stratton," Andrea said. "She trains my uncle's horses."

Mrs. Temple acknowledged Liz, then turned to greet another young girl carrying a cage of rabbits.

"How many different breeds are there?" Liz set the cage down on the concrete floor, gazing in amazement at the long lines of cages with hundreds of perky little bunnies in all sizes and colors pressing tiny noses to the wire.

That Winning Touch   77

"About forty," Andrea said. "I have to check in. There's Pete."

Liz wondered how anyone could make sense of all the confusion. What should she do now?

"Where do the rabbits go?" Liz asked Pete when all the traveling cages had been stacked against a wall.

"Match the ear tattoos to the cards over the exhibit cages. Here, I'll show you." Pete dragged a reluctant mini lop out by the scruff of its neck and showed the tattoo on the fleshy part of the ear. Then he instructed Liz how to hold one. "You grab the rabbit behind the ears, swing it up like this, and support its back with your arm."

Liz did as he instructed and was kicked in the side, then scratched. By the time she found the proper cage for the lop, blood trickled from a deep gouge running from wrist to elbow.

Liz found cages for four more rabbits. Another scratch, high on one arm from a collision with the open door of a cage, dripped more blood. Yet she felt quite proud of the fact that she'd learned to handle the rabbits easily enough.

She discovered she was hooked on rabbits. She loved the velvet fineness of their fur and their tiny little noses quivering with excitement. While Pete and Andrea put the traveling cages back in the truck, Liz wandered around, creating order from confusion after realizing the different categories of breeds were broken down into age, sex, and color.

"What type of rabbit is that?" She pointed at a tiny, round ball of fur nestled on a bed of pine chips.

Andrea giggled. "That's a cavy. You know, a guinea pig."

78   *That Winning Touch*

"You mean there are pedigreed guinea pigs too?" Liz laughed. The small animal skittered away. "This is too much for me. All I know are horses."

"We have to come back on Sunday. I do showmanship that day," Andrea said.

"Showmanship?"

Andrea headed back toward the rabbit section of the barn, Liz following. "It's a routine. The judge marks you on presentation, knowledge, and ability. It's kind of fun. I got a blue ribbon last year." Andrea waved at some friends. Pete announced that he had to go back to the lamb barn and disappeared through the crowd.

"Uncle Chance will probably forget about that too." Andrea sounded more woebegone; resigned acceptance replaced anger.

"He won't," Liz said. "Besides, I'll come Sunday. I want to see how your rabbits do in the judging." She heard someone say rabbits could be litter-trained like cats. How was such a task accomplished?

"You mean it?" Andrea asked excitedly.

Liz nodded. "Barring catastrophe." They left the barn and climbed back into the truck.

The return trip consisted of constant conversation on Andrea's part. She told Liz as much about rabbits as she could cram into the half hour it took to get home.

Back at the house, Liz returned the keys to Margie and went to her office, only to find Sam lounging in her chair.

She shoved his feet off her desk. "That was pretty slick of you, ignoring Chance's orders to get Andrea's animals to the fair."

Sam's feet hit the floor with a thud. Her shot in the dark hit home. He looked startled and guilty. Then his face became bland and unreadable, his eyes moving over

That Winning Touch 79

Liz, insultingly suggestive. He smelled of stale tobacco, sweat, and whiskey.

"If you were a little nicer to me. . . ." The suggestion hung in the air between them, open to interpretation.

"I think it's time to get back to work." Liz straightened a pile of papers. She was a neat person and hated untidiness. She was mildly annoyed when she realized the files were not in the proper order. Had Sam been snooping? Why?

"Work?" He glanced at the clock.

"I've been gone only two hours," she said quietly. "You can't possibly have forgotten about me in all that time."

"You think you're pretty sharp, don't you, missy?" Sam said with a snort.

"I would take it kindly if you would vacate my chair. I've got work to do." Liz crossed her arms over her chest, one foot tapping impatiently. Sam didn't frighten her.

"You aren't gonna last any longer than the rest just because you're a woman and the boss likes you."

"Are you threatening me?" Annoyance deepened into anger.

"I suppose you'll go complainin' about me to Chance?"

"I fight my own battles," she replied. "And I don't need Chance's protection. I don't know what game you're playing, but don't threaten me, Sam. You'll lose."

"Your job belongs to me." Sam pounded his fist on the desk. "I earned it. I know horses well enough—"

"You know them so well that when you took them to Santa Anita last winter you lost every race you entered," she finished for him sarcastically. "You didn't think I

80   *That Winning Touch*

knew, did you?'' Chance had given Sam an opportunity to show what he could do as trainer. He had failed miserably in the task. Liz had found out only by accident when she'd come across registration papers for a series of races. Sam had signed his name as trainer.

He glared at her and she glared back, hands on hips, her chin thrust forward. ''I could have done better if Chance had let me,'' he protested.

''He *did* let you.'' Her voice was cold and level.

He stalked out, slamming the door. Liz ignored him. She had too much on her mind to worry about him.

She shuffled the files back into order, extracting the bills—from the vet, feed store, and some equipment purchases. She unlocked the desk and drew out the ledgers and checkbook.

''Liz, I've found you. I've been all over!'' Margie puffed into the office, perspiring freely in the afternoon heat. She waved her apron at her flushed face and leaned against the door.

''What's the matter?'' Alarmed, Liz jumped to her feet and ran to the older woman to guide her to the chair.

''It's the toilet in the powder room,'' Margie said between gasps for breath. ''It's plugged again and overflowing all over the floor and through the hall.''

''Can't you call a plumber?'' Liz asked in exasperation.

''Chance said you were in charge,'' Margie said.

Liz sighed. Besides the horses, she had inherited the responsibility of the house and its occupants.

''You must have someone you call.'' What kind of damage was happening to the hall floor? Margie had such pride in the beautiful wood parquet. She hated to see it damaged.

That Winning Touch 81

"Yes, but. . . ."

"Go call," Liz said. "I'll assess the damage."

Margie rushed back toward the house. Liz followed several feet behind. She saw Allen and summoned him, explaining the situation as they hurried through the pool area, across the lawn, and into the house through the kitchen.

The hall qualified as a disaster area. Andrea was on her knees in an ever-increasing puddle of water, struggling to keep it from spreading with a pile of rags. Liz waded through the puddle, slipping as she walked into the powder room, and pulled the top off the tank. She couldn't see any problem. Finally she reached under the tank and turned the water off.

Andrea jumped up and slid toward the door of the little room. "No one could think how to turn the water off," she said.

"Margie's gone to call the plumber," Liz told her. "Find more towels. The water must be mopped up before it stains the floor and reaches the rugs in the living room."

Liz slid to the door and kicked back the nearest rug just as a runnel of water reached it. She grabbed a towel Allen tossed her and dropped it onto the floor, trying to create a barrier.

"The plumber says two hours, maybe more!" Margie wailed, grabbing at the wall to keep from slipping.

"The water's turned off," Liz said. "Let's get the floor mopped up."

"My beautiful floor!" Margie cried. She'd brought a mop and swished it through the puddle vigorously.

Liz dropped to her knees and started wiping up with towels. Allen rolled up the Navajo rugs that were in the most immediate danger, pushing them away as water flooded into the living room.

An hour later, Liz wearily sat on the floor surveying the damage. Some of the parquet tiles had curled. One tile looked as if it would have to be replaced. When the doorbell rang, Allen walked carefully across the wet floor and opened the door to the plumber.

"The commode's cracked," the plumber announced after making his inspection. "It's going to have to be replaced."

Liz passed a hand over her eyes. "Give me an estimate." She glanced at Andrea and found the girl with her hands clapped over her mouth to prevent giggles from escaping. Even Liz had to admit the whole situation had all the aspects of a Keystone Kops comedy. "I'll call Chance. I'll be in his office."

She walked into his office. The room, though neat, attested to Chance's abrupt departure. Papers on the desk had not been filed, and a tape recorder with a note attached to it sat on a corner.

She sat down at the desk and picked up the phone, pressing the code that automatically dialed Chance's office.

"Mr. Brentwood's office," the secretary's efficient voice answered. In the background, Liz could hear laughter.

"This is Liz Stratton. Is Mr. Brentwood available? It's an emergency." Her voice sounded hollow as she listened to it travel down the line. An echo came back to her.

"He's away from his office," the secretary said.

Quickly, Liz summarized the situation to the secretary, asking that Chance call back immediately.

"The floor is rotting out under the commode." The

That Winning Touch   83

plumber stood in the doorway to the office, lighting a cigarette.

"Anything else?" Liz asked, resigned to the fact that she would have to decide immediately without Chance's authorization.

He scratched his face and hitched up his overalls. "The pipes look all right."

"When can you start?"

"Tomorrow morning," he answered. "I'll have everything I need by then. I'll call you with an estimate this afternoon."

The phone rang and Liz picked it up.

"Hello, it's Chance." His voice sounded concerned.

She felt a pleasant rippling sensation. Quickly, she told him what had happened.

"You sound tired," he said.

"I've already had a long day," she replied. "Andrea thinks you forgot about her rabbits. And she was upset."

"I told Sam to ask you to take her to the fair."

"I'm not the same as you," she said. Sam had deliberately withheld the information of Chance's orders. She briefly considered telling Chance what Sam had done, but dismissed it. She could handle him.

A strained silence settled between them.

"I'll explain to her later," he said finally.

"Did you leave because of me? Because of what happened the other night?" She choked on the words. She still felt the confusion generated by his kiss.

"An emergency required my personal attention. I told Margie you were in charge, and you are. I'll see that enough funds are transferred to the household account for the repairs."

"Thank you." She glanced at the flashing digital clock

on his desk and saw it was nearly five o'clock. She rubbed her tired eyes, thinking of the chores left before she could rest.

"I'll be back as soon as I can," he assured her.

"Okay." She wanted him nearer than the other end of the phone, and she didn't understand why she felt this way.

"Liz, I. . . ." Chance paused. "I'll see you later."

She hung up the phone and wearily pulled herself to her feet. Then she and Allen went to feed the horses.

Chance hung up the phone. Across from him, Dicey Anderson studied her long, clawlike nails.

"You're looking great these days, Chance," she purred. She crossed her slim, shapely legs, hiking her skirt up over her knees. "Now tell me what's on your mind."

Chance had dated Dicey for a while, but no chemistry had exploded between them. She was a nice-enough person, but she had a passion for dangerous men, fast cars, and high living.

"I want to know about Liz Stratton," he said bluntly. There was no sense letting her think he planned to revive old times.

Dicey looked surprised. "Don't tell me you've fallen in love with her already."

"I want to know what happened to her. Who did she love who hurt her so badly?" The fear in Liz's eyes haunted him. For all her abilities and her stubborn persistence to establish herself as a trainer, she seemed so innocent at the game of love.

Dicey took a deep breath, a knowing look in her eyes. "All right. His name was Timmy Allanby. He worked

That Winning Touch   85

for her father and was just as mad about racing as Liz,
but for different reasons.'' Dicey squirmed uncomfortably in her chair.

Chance watched her. ''And what are those reasons?''

''Timmy is a very nasty man. He uses people, then
discards them. He wanted Liz to help him fix a race by
drugging a horse. You must remember the scandal. Liz
went to the track stewards and told them about Timmy's
plans.''

Dimly, Chance recalled hearing something that re-
sulted in a groom being barred from the track.

''I like Liz a lot,'' Dicey continued. ''I wish we could
be better friends. She's something quite unusual, and is
the only person who's never condemned me about the
type of men I like.'' Dicey leaned forward in her chair,
sounding and looking sincere, yet a small frown creased
her brows as if she were wondering how much she should
confide in him. ''Timmy Allanby has no morals and Liz
is the most honest person I've ever known.''

''I've become aware of that.''

Dicey took a deep breath. ''Don't hurt her, Chance. I
think that Liz is too naive for her own good. She expects
everyone in the world to act in the same ethical manner
she does. So take care.'' She stood and walked out of
the office, swaying so gracefully that Chance found himself admiring her poise and resolve.

Late in the evening, Liz dragged herself into her bedroom. She had one thing in mind: a swim in the pool to
relieve the tensions of the long day.

She pulled on her suit, grabbed a towel, and was out
the door in seconds. But her swim wouldn't feel right

86   *That Winning Touch*

with Chance gone. She searched the pool, half hoping he might be there, but the area was empty.

At the edge of the pool, she plunged into the heated water, the warmth embracing her, shielding her from the cool of the night. Demons had followed her throughout the day—little disturbances in her emotions that told her she missed Chance, while her mind tried to tell her she didn't. She'd been so careful since Timmy. How could she have let her guard down so easily?

As she swam, she came to understand that she enjoyed their meetings in the pool, away from the daily activities and the constant demands on their time. And she had come to enjoy their conversations, their analysis of the day behind them. In so short a time, Chance had sneaked under her defenses.

She swam to the edge of the pool, surfaced, caught the lip, and held on to it. A figure lounged in a chair. For a second, Liz's heart raced, and she thought Chance had returned. But the shadowy figure proved to be Jack. He moved into the sphere of light, which added unattractive hollows to his face.

" 'Evening,'' he said cordially, squatting next to her.

He wore too-tight bathing trunks. His body, soft and white with rolls of skin about the middle, was not her idea of a romantic figure. Even Timmy had been in better physical shape.

"All by yourself?'' he drawled with an innocent glance around the pool area. He sat on the edge of the pool and dangled his legs in the water. "Water's cold. How can you stand it?''

"What are you doing here?'' Incensed at having her peace disturbed, she glared at him.

"I have the use of the pool too,'' he said, his tone

That Winning Touch   87

unctuous. "Though I'd rather go dancing in Escondido. Do you like to dance?"

"Not particularly." How could she get rid of him?

"That's too bad. Why don't you let me take you to my favorite night spot and teach you?"

"No, thank you." Liz wanted to be alone so she could think about Chance—his craggy face and deep-set green eyes. She could picture the way his hair curled about his ears. She missed him, even though he'd been gone only a day.

"You think you're pretty special, don't you?" Jack said nastily. "Special enough to attract Chance's attention?"

"It's none of your business what I think of myself, or of Chance. You have only yourself to account for."

"And what does that mean?" His voice turned threatening.

"In case you've missed something, you happen to work for me, Jack." Her voice trembled with anger. "If you don't leave, you're going to find out what kind of temper I have."

Instead, he slid into the water. He grabbed at her before she could shove away from him. His fingers slid down her slippery skin and he went under. He grabbed at the edge of the pool and held on, watching helplessly as she hoisted herself out of the water and reached for the towel, wrapping it around her.

"You're fired," she said in a cold voice. "I want you off this property by morning."

"You can't fire me. Chance won't let you." Jack tried to pull himself out of the water, but found himself forced to use the ladder. He climbed out, water sluicing off him. He hitched up his suit.

88 *That Winning Touch*

"Chance left me in charge during his absence," She said, her voice frosty. She didn't know if she had the authority to fire him, but she intended to try.

"We'll just have to see about that." He grabbed her arm, his fingers digging into her flesh. "If I'm going to be fired anyway, it should be for a better reason than invading your precious swim time."

He wrestled her to him, his lips puckered to kiss her. She twisted out of his grasp. When he reached for her again, she slapped him. He stared at her, mouth agape like a suffocating fish.

"Do you think your daddy will intercede for you?" she asked.

"He'll call Chance and tell him all about you. You won't be here much longer." He pouted like a child, his cheeks puffed out and petulant chin tucked in.

"You have until tomorrow morning." Liz remained out of his reach. "If you're still here by the time morning practice is over, I'll have the police arrest you for trespassing."

"You can't do that." His shrill voice bounded off the water and echoed through the night.

"I just did." Liz stalked off without looking back. She'd had enough of Jack and his adolescent personality. It was time for him to grow up.

She entered her apartment and locked the outside door. Stripping off her suit, she stepped into the shower. Refreshed, she climbed into bed and composed herself for sleep. But sleep was elusive. Instead, she kept seeing Chance—at the fair, watching the horses, sitting by the pool in the moonlight.

That Winning Touch 89

She twisted and turned in the bed until the sheets tangled around her legs. Finally, she fell into a restless slumber, her dreams chaotic, full of disjointed images and flaring emotions.

Chapter Six

As abruptly as he left, Chance returned. Leaning over the rail of the fence surrounding the exercise track on Saturday morning, Liz felt someone watching her. She looked around and saw Chance walking toward her, using his cane to balance on the uneven ground.

A four-year-old gelding named Shay's Pride circled the track. A handsome roan with a long neck and proudly held head, he nipped at Silverado's rump, earning a sideways kick. Andrea flicked the end of her whip at Shay's Pride's cheek. Allen drew Silverado away. The horses were in fine fettle this morning. She hoped they'd take that energy to Del Mar.

She signaled Allen and Andrea. Silverado sprinted. Andrea slapped Shay's Pride. The two horses raced around the track.

Liz clicked the stopwatch in her hand, watching the second hand move swiftly around the face. When she stopped it, she waved at Allen, who eased Silverado into an easy canter and then to a walk. Andrea strained to stop Shay's Pride, but the big horse wanted to keep running. Finally, she let him continue around the track until some of his energy abated.

By the time Allen and Silverado approached the fence,

90

That Winning Touch   91

Chance was standing next to Liz. He reached out to pat the fine head of the animal while she recorded the times in her notebook. She smiled at Allen, then waved at Kippy Marshall, who was mounted on Ayala. Kippy was fourteen years old, and helped exercise the thoroughbreds in return for stable privileges for his own horse.

Kippy approached the marking post. Ayala sprinted. Liz started the watch. The horse streaked past her, neck out, head reaching forward. She was a beautiful animal, her coat shining in the morning light. Liz still hoped to race her at Del Mar.

The watch clicked off and she waved at Kippy, who pulled on the reins, easing the animal into a canter and then into a long-strided walk. Andrea fought Shay's Pride to a standstill at the fence. She glared at her uncle, giving him no greeting, her face set into stubborn lines of anger.

"How are they doing?" Chance asked. He scratched Shay's Pride's velvety chin.

"Just fine." Liz grabbed the reins and held Shay's Pride while Andrea continued to glare at her uncle. Liz gestured to Allen to walk Silverado around the track, cooling the animal after the workout. "Silverado made good time just now." She showed Chance her notebook.

"Will you take him to Del Mar?" He leaned against the fence.

"I'm thinking about it."

"You're back," Andrea stated in a flat voice. She patted Shay's Pride automatically, her hand lingering lovingly on the silken mane.

Liz winced at the harshness of her voice.

She told Kippy to cool Ayala and put her away. Then she turned to Chance and Andrea.

N. A.

92   *That Winning Touch*

"Yes, I'm back," he said with a wary glance at his niece.

Liz ducked through the fence rails, realizing that Chance and Andrea had a few things to talk about. She helped Andrea to the ground and then mounted in her place. She drew Shay's Pride away from the fence for a cooling walk around the track. The horse had a hard mouth. He played constantly with the bit.

"That doesn't look good back there." Allen jerked his thumb at Chance and Andrea when Liz joined him.

Shay's Pride fought Liz. Her arms began to feel as if they'd be pulled out of their sockets.

"They have to settle it," she responded. The horse quivered under her, anticipating another run, his energy level still high. Liz talked in a soothing voice. She didn't want to be riding away from Chance. She wanted to be near to him. But Andrea had a prior claim.

Sam stood to one side, casually smoking a cigarette. Liz motioned to him, insisting he put out the cigarette. The ground underfoot was tinder-dry. A fire could start easily.

"And then it will be your turn," Allen said.

"I don't have to explain to him why I fired Jack. He left me in charge, and Jack overstepped his limits." Yet Liz was worried. Would Chance be angry over Jack's dismissal? He'd asked her to be diplomatic with Sam, and she'd started a war.

Sam had made no fuss over the situation. But Liz could feel the vicious fury building in the older man just below the surface. He doted on his son too much.

"Sam isn't going to let it rest." Silverado danced briefly and Allen brought him back to a walk.

Both horses were charged, the love of racing bred into

That Winning Touch   93

them. Silverado and Shay's Pride knew they were going back to the track to race. In three weeks Del Mar would open, beginning the racing season at one of the most beautiful tracks on the West Coast.

Liz and Allen walked the horses around the track several times, careful to avoid Chance and Andrea. When Liz judged the argument to be over, she slid from the saddle and handed the reins to Allen with orders to walk the animals for another half hour. Then she headed back to Chance, her long-legged stride taking her across the track in seconds.

Andrea was gone. Chance leaned against the top rail of the fence, a brooding expression on his face.

"I assume you're going to want to talk to me too." Liz felt an electric awareness of him move through her, a sudden jump in her pulses as she ached to smooth away the worry on his face. They turned from the fence and headed back toward the barns.

"Is there something I don't know?" He stumbled and used the cane to catch himself.

Liz slowed her pace. She bit the inside of her lip, wondering if Sam had called Chance to complain about her. Sam seemed to waste no opportunities in trying to make her look irresponsible and careless.

"It's about Jack," she said.

Chance sighed. She could see that he already knew, and she fell silent. She owed him no explanation, but Sam was Chance's longtime friend. Chance deserved to hear her reasons.

"What happened?" His cane sank into a soft spot and he stopped to pull it free.

"Jack behaved inappropriately." She flinched at the look of pain crossing his face. "And I fired him."

94 *That Winning Touch*

In her office, Liz poured two cups of coffee and handed one to him. She sipped her coffee as she gave him a rundown of the events of the last several days.

The powder room in the front hall was still out of commission. The plumber had promised to have the job done by Saturday, but once the floor had been torn up, he'd found rot in the framing. Liz had to arrange for a construction company to come in and finish the job.

Chance listened, studying Liz until her voice faltered and trailed away.

"You did fine." He ran his hand over his face and pushed the hair away from his forehead.

"I didn't know I was going to be responsible for the household as well as the stable. Actually, I had fun," she admitted.

She had enjoyed her brief moment of power when she called the different companies to make arrangements for written estimates, arguing pleasantly with contractors, trying to get the best price for the repair work. She had expanded her horizons somewhat in dealing with people who had no connection whatever with racing, and she felt good about it, She was slowly realizing that the whole world did not revolve around the racetrack.

Chance smiled at her and she smiled back. "You look like you enjoyed yourself," he said. "Thank you for taking care of everything. So, tell me about Del Mar."

That question never went away. Everyone's curiosity about Del Mar made Liz smile. She quickly outlined the developments in the animals. Silverado's time was improving and she thought he'd be ready for Del Mar. She'd decided against Deadly Justice. His sore hoof had flared into an infection, and she'd made an emergency call to

That Winning Touch   95

the stable vet, Jilla Markham, who dosed him with antibiotics and told her to continue the poultices.

"You're not going to take just Silverado, are you?" Chance asked curiously.

"I've decided on five horses," Liz said. "Silverado, Ayala, Betsy Ross, and Shay's Pride." She hadn't settled on the fifth horse yet. Prime Mover had been worked hard and showed promise. "I have to admit, considering the fragility of the breed, your thoroughbreds are remarkably healthy. They've had few minor injuries. You've been lucky."

"I don't keep any that are prone to trouble," Chance answered. He took a sip from his cup and told her she made excellent coffee.

"I didn't make it," Liz admitted. "Allen did."

Chance laughed. "Can you cook?" he asked curiously.

"A little." She wasn't courageous enough to tell him how little. She'd never been interested in cooking or anything considered one of the "womanly arts." Her father had tried to direct her toward more feminine pursuits, but she'd managed to avoid them as much as possible.

"I told Sam I support your decision about Jack," Chance said, the weary look returning to his eyes.

"I'm sorry if I've caused a problem." Her apology was the closest thing to admitting that she might have been hasty. Yet she couldn't have Jack constantly questioning her authority or trying to kiss her because she wasn't easily attainable.

"No." Chance rubbed his eyes. "Jack's been trouble for a long time. He needs to find out what the world's like without his father's largess. You did right. Now, tell me what to do with Andrea."

96   *That Winning Touch*

Liz hadn't expected this question. What should she say? "Andrea loves you. She just wants you to spend more time with her, pay attention to her. She's entering a terribly confusing time in her life. She needs your guidance."

"I'm not much of a mother," Chance said. Then he added in a rueful tone, "Her own mother isn't much of a mother, either."

Liz couldn't understand why Susanna wasn't as enchanted with Andrea as she was. Liz adored the girl, seeing in Andrea her own youthful self. "Just do what you think is right, Chance," she concluded.

At any rate, his problems with his niece were his business. She was hardly in a position to advise him. Her own troubles with her father had gone unresolved until the day of his death. Yet she'd never doubted his love and concern for her. Andrea didn't seem to know how much Chance loved her.

"She admires you, Liz."

"I'm not a substitute."

He pushed himself to his feet, shaking his head. "I can deal with the most temperamental client, but not Andrea. If only her parents. . . ." His voice trailed away, the responsibility he had assumed seeming like a gigantic obstacle.

Liz watched him limp out of the office, her heart going out to him. She wanted to run after him and tell him she was sorry she couldn't make the world a better place. Instead, she opened her account book.

"Hello, Liz." Dicey Anderson walked into the office. Her skirt billowed as she sat down on the empty chair. Her perfume filled the room. Liz sneezed. "I thought I'd find you here."

That Winning Touch   97

"What are you doing here?" Liz asked. She'd known Dicey for years.

"Chance invited me for the Fourth of July weekend. Didn't he tell you? He's invited several people. We're all going to have a marvelous time." She smiled.

Liz thought of a rude comment, but refrained from using it. Dicey Anderson was all right, but Liz had never cared to be around her. She ran with a fast crowd of racing enthusiasts who left their common sense at the gate and gambled themselves into bankruptcy at the big money windows.

"Besides," Dicey continued, "why should you have a clear field to Chance Brentwood? I came because I thought you needed a little competition."

Liz burst out laughing. In all the years she'd known Dicey, she never thought of her as competition. How could Liz ever compete with the artificial perfection of Dicey Anderson? Dicey, with her beautifully coiffed head, perfect complexion, and fashion-slim body. There was no comparison.

"You always have had a way of deflating people," Dicey said in an aggrieved tone.

"I'm sorry. It's just hard to think of you as competing with me. We're so different." Liz realized this was the first time she'd laughed in days. "You make me feel as if I'm the most naive person in the world. But never as competition."

"You *are* the most naive person in the world." Dicey joined in the laughter, hers a tinkling octave of high notes.

"I had no idea Chance was bringing a party back from Los Angeles," Liz said, wondering how the group of people would affect the schedule of the stable. She hated disruption.

98   *That Winning Touch*

"Just a few friends," Dicey replied. "And I'd be truly honored if *we* could be friends."

Before Liz could answer, a man entered, saying, "Here you are, Dicey. I've been looking all over for you."

Dicey stood in a lithe, supple movement and went to the man who shadowed the door. She draped herself around him like a cat.

Liz stared. Her mouth dropped open and she blinked.

"Paul Chambers," Dicey purred, "this is Liz Stratton. I told you about her. She's very knowledgeable about racehorses."

"Hello, Liz." Paul held out a hand. He was about forty years old, with pale brown hair graying at the temples and piercingly direct blue eyes that looked Liz over quickly, then dismissed her to gaze adoringly at Dicey.

Liz shook his hand, surprised at the strength. Dicey usually had an eye for lifeguards with biceps on their triceps. This man was definitely not a beach puppy. His body was round and plump, but the tone of his arms told her he'd once been a muscular man. He had a nice smile.

"Hello," she said, finally finding her voice.

"You're prettier than Dicey led me to believe. Why is that, darling?" he asked Dicey with a fond smile.

She actually blushed. She stared at her hands and bit her lips. Watching Liz, her eyes pleaded with some unknown message.

"Dicey isn't always generous with her descriptions." Liz tempered her remark with a slight smile. He nodded in understanding.

Dicey groaned, looking as if she wanted to cry.

"It's all right." Paul slid his arms around Dicey and kissed the top of her head. "We're only teasing."

Liz marveled that anyone who knew Dicey—with her

That Winning Touch 99

temper tantrums and her vicious love of gossip—could possibly love her. Yet Paul seemed to have exactly that feeling for Dicey. And from the look on her face, Dicey had finally fallen in love. For some reason, Liz felt excited that Dicey had found a purpose—and depressed because she herself still felt so empty.

"Will we see you at dinner?" Paul asked.

"I don't know," Liz replied. "I'm only an employee here."

Paul's gentle smile told her he didn't quite believe her. But he nodded and drew Dicey away. Liz sat down hard on her desk, grabbing at the edge, too amazed to even think.

The remainder of the day passed slowly. Liz forgot lunch, so Margie brought her a sandwich and snack on a tray. Liz didn't want to meet Chance's guests, who, she assumed, included some of the most glamorous women in Los Angeles.

"Liz?" Looking very worried, Barbie Wilton entered. Late-afternoon shadows stretched across the ground.

"What is it?" she asked, alarmed. Barbie was fifteen years old and stabled a mare in the last barn.

"It's my horse." Barbie burst into tears. "Could you look at her? I don't know what's wrong."

Liz had no responsibility for the privately owned horses in the stable, but she couldn't deny Barbie's request when she looked so frightened.

She found Barbie's small half-Morgan and half-Arab mare wandering restlessly about her stall, panting heavily, her rounded sides heaving with effort.

Liz walked into the stall and touched the animal's head. The mare rolled her eyes at her. She patted her reassuringly.

100 *That Winning Touch*

"How old is she?" she asked, checking the animal over carefully, already knowing the problem.

"She's seventeen." Barbie patted her horse.

"Has she ever foaled before?"

"No, never."

"Have you ever seen a mare in labor?" Liz asked. She couldn't help the faint laugh that escaped her lips. She turned it into a cough, knowing how sensitive young girls could be about their horses.

Barbie ran around the animal and stared at Liz. "But . . . but . . ." she spluttered helplessly.

The mare strained hard, her head stretched out toward the door. The contraction ended and she resumed her aimless walking.

"Go and get the foaling box," Liz said. "It's in my office."

Barbie disappeared and Liz patted the horse. The animal nosed at her hand. Occasionally, she turned her head to look at her flanks.

Barbie rushed back, too breathless to speak. She set the foaling box on the floor and then stared at her horse in amazement. "What's happened?"

"Nothing yet. It's going to be a while," Liz soothed the girl. "Why don't you call your parents? Tell them what's happening and that you're going to be late."

"I don't understand," Barbie said with a confused shake of her head.

"Well, I do," Liz said, trying not to laugh. "Every spring you pasture your mare, the last two with Pete's stallion."

"I thought that Misty was too old. And Pete's stallion is nearly twenty-six."

"You obviously thought wrong." A laugh finally escaped at the incredulous look on Barbie's face. "Go telephone your parents. They'll worry if you're not home in time for dinner."

Barbie dashed off again. Liz leaned against the wall. The mare scratched her side against a wall brace and sniffed without interest at her water trough.

Liz had little to do except watch her. Nature had her own competent schedule and didn't need much outside assistance.

When Barbie returned, Liz telephoned Jilla Markham, the stable vet, to ask her to have someone on standby just in case. The mare was seventeen and having her first foal. The birth would probably progress normally, but Liz believed in being prepared for any emergency.

After a short conversation with the veterinarian, Liz called the house and told Margie not to set a place for her at dinner. She explained about Barbie's mare and asked for sandwiches to be brought to the barn.

Liz returned to the stall to find Misty on the ground breathing heavily. After a few moments, the mare got to her feet again and continued her restless wandering around the stall.

"Isn't there anything I can do?" Barbie asked anxiously.

"Nothing." Liz slid her arm around the girl and hugged her, remembering when life was so innocently simple.

"Is she all right?"

"Misty is older and hasn't been terribly active the last few years. She'll probably have a long labor, but she's fine."

"I didn't even notice," Barbie said in wonderment.

"What would you have noticed? It takes an experi-

102   *That Winning Touch*

enced horseman to see the signs and interpret them correctly. I didn't see them myself.'' Liz sat in the straw and patted the spot next to her. After a few seconds, Barbie joined her.

"How long will it take?'' she asked curiously. "I've never seen a foal being born.''

Liz shrugged. "It depends. You stay with her. I'm going to check my horses. I'll be back in a few minutes.''

She made her nightly rounds, encountering Allen and Kippy doing the night feeding. She told them what was happening. Allen hid his laughter behind a forkful of hay.

She visited each stall. She patted the animals and spoke to them. Chance had some of the best-behaved thoroughbreds she had ever seen. For the most part, they were even-tempered and calm. She had come to love them all, from the more nervous Shay's Pride to the majestically noble Silverado.

"I understand we have an event happening in the other barn,'' Chance said, joining Liz as she patted Silverado.

"Yes, a slight miscalculation on Barbie's part. She thought Pete's stallion was too old to beget future generations.'' Liz found herself laughing again.

"Wait till she's been married forty years and she'll find nothing is ever 'too old.' '' Chance joined in the laughter. The lines disappeared from his face.

Liz wanted to tell him that she was glad he was back from Los Angeles and that she'd missed him and their nightly swims. But she didn't. She stood slightly away from him, conscious of his nearness.

Her arm brushed his and he turned to look at her. "About last Sunday . . .'' she began.

"You don't have to apologize,'' he said softly.

"You don't understand.'' An edge of desperation in-

That Winning Touch 103

vaded her voice. "And now isn't the time to explain. I told Barbie I'd be right back. She's frightened. It's her mare's first foal."

They walked down the feed alley and out into the evening shadows. "If you need the vet. . . ."

"I've already put her on alert. The mare's seventeen and it could be a long night." Liz sobered at the thought of all that could go wrong. "I'm not too good at emergency surgery."

"I'll have Margie fill the large thermos with hot coffee."

"Thank you." She suddenly felt good, knowing he was near. For a moment, she thought he would kiss her, but he didn't.

"I'll check back with you later." He headed toward the house while Liz turned toward her office.

When she entered, she found Sam searching her desk. He jumped when she walked in.

"What are you looking for?" Liz demanded. "If you intend to try discrediting me with Chance in the way you got rid of Judd, forget it. I keep excellent records of every penny I spend and ask for complete receipts from the merchants."

For a second, Sam looked confused. Then he growled, shoved past her, and disappeared into the night.

Liz leaned against the wall, fighting hard for breath. Until Sam had left, she hadn't felt particularly scared. Suddenly, she was terrified. He hated her. She had seen the look on his face. What would he do?

She closed her office and locked the door for the first time since her arrival at Brentwood Farms. She headed back to Barbie, ignoring the weakness in her knees.

Misty lay in the straw with her neck stretched out and

104   *That Winning Touch*

breathing with her mouth open. When she relaxed after the contraction, Liz took the chance to check her, making certain the delivery was proceeding normally. She patted the sleek neck.

"Is something wrong?" Barbie sat on the ground, hugging her knees to her chest.

"Nothing's wrong." Liz wrapped the tail in a tail bandage and then gently washed the birth area. She checked the mare swiftly and stepped back as Misty pulled herself up to her feet and began to pace restlessly around the stall area again.

"But you're not doing anything." Barbie wrapped and rewrapped her arms around her knees.

"Misty is doing everything herself." Liz pushed hair out of her face. She kicked the foaling box to a corner and sat down.

"What happens now?" Barbie asked.

"We wait." Liz grinned. "Do you want a soda?"

"All right." Barbie jumped to her feet.

"She's as nervous as most fathers." Chance stood in the door, a huge thermos under his arm. He handed it to Liz.

"It's an event for her," she said. "The first time I saw a foal being born, I was eleven. It was a marvelous thing then—and still wonderful now."

She scrambled to her feet, brushing straw off her jeans. She joined Chance outside the stall, standing in the feed alley and turning to watch the mare. A feeling of contentment crept over her. She smiled at Chance and he smiled in return.

"I hate to have to leave."

"But you have a houseful of guests."

He shrugged. "I'll be back when I can."

That Winning Touch   105

"He's nice," Barbie said, watching Chance limp across the landscaped area toward the fence surrounding the pool. "If he didn't let me stable Misty here, I wouldn't have any place to keep her. My mother didn't want me to have a horse."

"Mothers are like that sometimes." Liz's mother had died so young, she only had the haziest memory of her. She recalled a light floral perfume and a musical laugh and nothing else.

"I guess so," Barbie replied, unconvinced.

Andrea arrived with a basket of food over her arm. She wore a blue party dress with a lace collar. Her hair, brushed back from her face, was secured with two flowered pins.

"I wish I could watch," she said, looking at the mare wistfully. "But Uncle Chance says I'm hostess tonight. Margie packed enough food for an army. You won't be hungry."

"I hope not." Liz took the basket and peeked inside. Margie had outdone herself, with deep-fried chicken, tossed green salad, herb-seasoned green beans, and two large, ripe apples.

"I'm not hungry," Barbie said.

"I don't believe that." Liz laughed. "We'll sit out here in the alley where we can see Misty. I'm starved. I seem to be forever missing lunch and even dinner."

Andrea grinned. "Margie says you don't eat enough."

"She's probably right."

"I have to go." Andrea sighed. "Will you wake me and tell me when the foal is born, no matter what time it is?"

"If the birth is early enough," Liz said. "Otherwise, you'll have to wait till morning."

106   *That Winning Touch*

After Andrea left, they sat on the ground, spreading a cloth over the dirt and setting out two place mats, napkins, and plates. Liz portioned out the food and watched the not-so-hungry Barbie demolish three pieces of chicken, a huge helping of salad, and both apples.

"It's taking so long." Barbie's head swiveled toward the stall. She flinched in sympathy as the mare thrashed.

Liz didn't think labor would be much longer. Her watch showed nine o'clock, less than three hours since Barbie had first come for her. She could hear the restless stamping of the horses in the side stalls.

She reassured Barbie and leaned back against the door, her thoughts randomly moving from Chance to Timmy, then to herself and back to Chance.

The floodlights over the pool area flashed on. She listened to faint laughter intermingled with frenzied splashing, wishing she could enjoy a refreshing swim.

Misty panted and strained, perspiring heavily. Liz thought of Chance and the troubled emotions he roused in her, not understanding why she fought the tentative blossom of love he offered her. A part of her desperately wanted to give in, but another part of her stood aloof and cold, not wanting to be in so vulnerable a position again, or to be hurt.

Shortly after ten o'clock, the mare lay down for the final time, her neck arched, hooves pawing the straw.

"Something's happening!" Barbie cried out excitedly.

Liz knelt in the straw, watching in fascination as a tiny hoof protruded from the birth canal. A small quivering nose followed. The mare strained mightily, her panting filling the stall. Another contraction occurred and the head popped out, followed by the shoulders, the hips, and the hind legs.

That Winning Touch
107

"Oh!" Barbie breathed in astonishment. She jumped back in surprise as the limp little body rolled across the straw.

Liz reached for her foaling box, throwing it open and grabbing for the iodine. The umbilical cord snapped as the foal rocked away from the mare. Quickly, she dipped the end of the cord into the iodine, then stepped back again.

The mare relaxed on the straw for a long moment, her beautiful coat bathed in sweat. She took several deep breaths, then pulled herself to her feet. She nosed the wet bundle in the straw and placidly began licking away the birth membrane.

"What is it?" Barbie asked.

"It's a filly," Liz answered. She moved away from the foal, leaving her to her mother's ministrations, and then checked the mare. "Come and take a look, but move slowly and carefully. You don't want to alarm Misty."

Misty wasn't in the least aware of Liz and Barbie. She continued to carefully clean her newborn, nuzzling the filly, who struggled to gain purchase with her long, spindly legs.

"Barbie," Liz said softly, aware of the miracle of birth and its affect on the girl, "we'll need fresh straw. Why don't you get some? The stall should be cleaned as soon as Misty's foal is on her feet."

While Barbie ran toward the storage barn, Liz looked around for a blanket. The mare needed to be dried off. She saw Chance watching her.

"Have you been here long?" Jubilation sounded in her voice. An old blanket hung on a nail in the alley and she began rubbing down the mare with it.

"Yes," he answered. "You were so wrapped up in

the foal you never noticed me. This has been an interesting evening.''

''It's been a wonderful evening.'' Liz laughed joy-
ously.

The foal struggled to her feet, rocking and rolling in
the hay, thrashing about with legs that seemed much too
long for her fragile little body.

''She seems to be reasonably alert.'' Chance grabbed
a cloth and helped Liz rub down the wet mare.

''Healthy newborn foals usually are. Soon she'll be on
her feet and ready to eat.''

Barbie returned, pushing a wheelbarrow with two bales
of straw balanced on it. Liz found Misty's blanket and
covered the horse.

''Should I start cleaning out now?'' Barbie asked, a
fearful tone in her voice as she gazed at the foal. The
filly had managed to get to her feet, then immediately
toppled over. Misty nosed her foal again.

''No, not until the foal's on her feet.'' Liz stepped
away from Misty and moved toward the door, her arm
brushing Chance's. An electric shock raced through her.
She looked up at him and saw that he'd reacted to her as
strongly as she to him.

The foal gained her feet and tottered on wobbling legs
toward her mother before collapsing in the straw again.
Liz chuckled and Barbie laughed.

''Should I help her up?'' Barbie asked.

''You have to let her find her feet on her own,'' Liz
said. ''It's nature's way of strengthening her muscles. In
the wild a foal has to be ready to run in only a few hours.''

By eleven o'clock, the foal was on her feet and tottering
uncertainly toward the source of her food. The mare dain-
tily guided her newborn. While the foal eagerly nursed,

That Winning Touch   109

Liz explained how to remove the soiled straw and set down fresh.

"I'll help," Chance said, rolling up his sleeves and grabbing a rake.

"Can you manage?" Liz looked at his leg, and he smiled at her.

"I can get around. I use the cane only because it makes walking easier. Without it, I'm just slower."

The three cleaned the stall and scattered fresh bedding. Liz remembered the vet and went to her office to call and announce the newest arrival at Brentwood Farms. She returned to the stall, where the soiled straw was piled in the wheelbarrow, ready to be dumped.

"The vet will come around tomorrow afternoon to check Misty out," Liz announced.

"Is everything all right?" Barbie asked in alarm. She dropped her rake, startling the foal, who fell to her knees and rolled over to lay panting in the straw, her huge brown eyes staring accusingly at Barbie. She giggled.

In a soothing tone, Liz said, "It's just a precaution."

"Everything here is under control," Chance said. "I'll drive you home, Barbie. Your parents must be worrying about you."

"Thank you, Mr. Brentwood, but I have to finish cleaning."

"I'll do it," Liz said. "You're tired. We're all tired. You can come back in the morning and drool over your new baby."

Liz closed the Dutch doors, satisfied that all was well inside. It was almost midnight. She groaned. In another four hours, she'd be up seeing to morning exercise. No sleep tonight.

She guided the wheelbarrow outside. Then she went

110   *That Winning Touch*

toward the house, her feet dragging. She stopped at the
pool to look at the crystal-clear water lit from the bottom.

The floodlights had been turned off long ago. The
guests who'd frolicked earlier had gone to bed. She
thought of her promise to Andrea, but found herself unwilling to disturb her.

She ached for the feel of the cool water against the
fevered warmth of her skin. She didn't have the energy.
Abruptly, she sat down on the side of the pool and stared
at the water.

Chance returned fifteen minutes later to find Liz sitting
on the edge of the pool, her shoes and socks in a pile
next to her, jeans rolled up over her knees. She hung her
feet in the water. She looked exhausted.

"Do you want to talk about it?" he asked.

"About what?" Liz barely glanced at him.

"About what's been troubling you?" He put a hand
on her shoulder.

She shrugged. "I don't know."

"You look like you could use a hot meal."

"I need to get to bed." She pulled her feet from the
water.

"My mother used to say that food is the greatest solace
in life."

Liz glanced up at him. "Maybe Margie has some food
left over from dinner."

"Maybe she does, but I have something different in
mind." He helped her to her feet. "I know a great little
restaurant on the beach that's open until two A.M., and
serves the best lobster this side of Maine."

Liz looked tempted, and Chance pressed his advantage.
She conceded, picking up shoes and socks to follow him
to the car.

That Winning Touch 111

The Surfside was Chance's favorite restaurant in Del Mar. It boasted a bank of windows overlooking the beach. Incoming surf pounded against sand and rocks used as a break to keep the tide from overflowing the dining area. The owner graciously led them to a choice table and seated Liz with a flourish.

Every table had a flickering candle that barely lit the eating area, a camellia floating in water, and large napkins wrapped around banged and dented eating utensils.

"This place certainly has atmosphere." Liz shook out her napkin.

"I like it." Chance ordered club soda for himself, and Liz asked for a glass of water with lemon. He leaned his elbows on the table and watched as she sipped the water.

The waitress set a basket of bread on the table, but Liz looked at it with little interest. Chance ordered lobster for both of them, then buttered a crisp sourdough slice.

"You want to tell me what's on your mind?" he coaxed, hoping she'd share her burden.

She watched the ocean. The moon, a golden crescent, lit the water with eerie enchantment. Waves rippled as they moved toward shore. Beyond the breakwater, a boat bobbed up and down.

Liz took a deep breath. "I feel I should apologize for my behavior Sunday night."

"That's old news." He brushed aside her apology.

"I knew someone once." She continued to gaze out at the ocean, as if afraid to look at him. "I thought I loved him. He was full of dreams and shared my love for racing."

Chance watched a play of emotions twist her face. The memories weren't pleasant, nor were they welcome. He

112   *That Winning Touch*

saw torment in her eyes and wanted to fix everything for her so that she could be happy.

Liz continued, "I thought he wanted what I wanted. I was so dazzled by him that I refused to see that he was trouble."

"We all fall in love, Liz. Love blinds even the best of us."

She shook her head. "Not like this. You see, Timmy had a plan." She turned to face him, a slight smile on her lips. "He said he needed me to give him some very special help." Her eyes filled with tears.

Chance wanted to touch her, to tell her she'd be all right. But he didn't, afraid that if he stopped her, she'd never start again. He felt jealous of the unknown man she'd once loved. "Go on," he said instead.

"Timmy's plan was actually quite clever. He was a smart man. My father trusted him. I thought I could trust him too, but after I thought about what Timmy wanted to do, I knew I couldn't let him destroy another man's good reputation. So I went to the track stewards and reported Timmy's get-rich-quick plan."

Chance heard the anguish, the pain in her voice. His fingers slid around her ice-cold ones. "You were in love. People in love do a lot of things they wouldn't do under more normal circumstances."

"You don't understand." She drew her hand away. "You see, I seriously thought about helping him, about the money we'd have. My father and I never had much money until I was in high school. We slept in tack rooms because we had no place else to sleep. I didn't want to live that way with Timmy. I almost helped him fix a race. If he'd succeeded, my father would have been banned from racing." Her voice caught on a sob.

That Winning Touch 113

"But you didn't. Your father raised you to be honest and ethical. . . ."

"In my heart, I didn't want to be honest and ethical. I wanted to be financially solvent."

Tears overflowed her eyes and tracked down her cheeks. Chance wiped them away with the corner of his napkin. "I suppose everyone entertains the idea of the perfect crime, a way to get money without having to work for it."

"I didn't like myself for a long time afterward because of what I was capable of doing to my own father. I had actually considered betraying him in a way that would have ruined him."

Chance grasped her hand and tugged it sharply to get her attention. "No one can be convicted for thinking. The important thing is your upbringing won over greed."

"I saw a part of myself I didn't know existed." She stared back at the ocean. Spray misted the windows.

The waitress appeared with their lobsters, and Chance attacked his as if he hadn't eaten in days. He hadn't paid any attention to his dinner, as his guests had kept him distracted all evening. He had found himself wondering why he'd invited them. True, the invitation had been a long-standing one, but he could have canceled.

"Everybody in the world harbors parts of their personality that aren't as nice as they think," he said. "We all have a dark side that I believe helps make us stronger and more capable of surviving. When that dark side turns up, we're always the first ones to be surprised at its existence."

"My dark side isn't pretty."

"Neither is mine."

Liz looked surprised. She neatly speared a chunk of

lobster and popped it into her mouth without dipping it in the clarified butter on her plate. The candles flickered, throwing her face in shadow, highlighting her cheekbones. Chance had never met a woman like Liz before. He'd spent years building his practice in Los Angeles, being seen in the right places with the right people. He'd dated women so breathtakingly beautiful even he was awed by them. Liz was different. She was totally unconscious of her appearance, unaware of her beauty. A piece of straw tangled with a red curl. Her eyes were hooded and thoughtful.

Chance felt the first flicker of genuine love for her. She was poised, self-possessed, and attractive in a way he'd never encountered before. She knew what she wanted, and he had to convince her that she wanted to be loved by him.

"Want to walk on the beach?" he asked when she'd finished her meal and pushed her plate away.

She glanced at her watch and frowned. "It's after one in the morning. I have to be up at four to exercise the horses."

"I know." He paid the bill and used his cane to stand up. "They're my horses, and Sam is capable of exercising them while you sleep in."

"I don't know." She walked ahead of him out of the restaurant to the parking lot. She glanced at the beach and the enticing expanse of sand.

Without another word, Chance guided her toward it. A path led down to the beach. She walked down it, her hair lit by the radiant beams of the moon.

Waves pounded the sand. Chance tasted salt on his tongue. He loved the ocean, the wild exuberance of it. As a child, he'd played on this same stretch of beach,

That Winning Touch   115

gathering seashells and tiny pebbles scoured smooth by the tides. He'd stood on the bluff above with binoculars and watched the annual migration of the gray whales. He'd once thought about studying oceanography, but had decided on law instead.

Liz found a bench and sat down. He sat with her.

"It's so peaceful here," she said with a low sigh. An ocean breeze stirred the ends of her long hair. She leaned against Chance's arm and closed her eyes.

He wanted the moment to go on and on, so he could keep savoring the peace, the warmth of her body, the floral fragrance of her hair. Finally, she stirred and stood up. She yawned.

"Thank you for the lobster and all this." She waved her hand at the ocean. "But I'd like to go before I fall asleep standing up."

Chance drove Liz home. He walked her to her door, but when he reached out to draw her into his arms, she slipped away and started to close the door firmly. "Liz," he said, "nothing is ever so awful that it can't be fixed."

"Good night, Chance," he heard through the door as he turned away and headed toward his own distant section of the house.

Chapter Seven

LIZ woke to predawn blackness. She rolled over, rubbing her eyes. Two hours of sleep. She'd managed on less, but paid a steep price.

Without turning on a light, she rummaged in the darkness for her clothes and let herself out into the chill morning air, pulling on a sweatshirt as she walked toward the stables. Kippy was saddling the horses. Andrea led the animals down the feed alley, a sullen look on her face.

"I'll ride Shay's Pride," Liz told Kippy as she entered her office. Allen came in, cradling a hot mug of coffee in his hands, warming his face over the rising steam. Liz poured a mug for herself.

" 'Morning," he said between sips. "Looks like it's going to be a nice day."

"Are you coming to my showmanship competition today?" Andrea stood in the door, Betsy Ross on a lead rein behind her.

"I intend to come." Liz sipped her coffee. She rubbed at her eyes, aware the lack of sleep would soon catch up with her.

Outside, the movements of the animals finally dragged

116

That Winning Touch   117

her away from her coffee. As she walked out the door she envisioned a day of caffeine to keep her awake.

Liz checked each animal every morning, running her hands down their legs, feeling the structure of their muscles and bones. She listened to their breathing, checked their temperature, and plotted the recovery of injuries.

The condition of each animal determined what exercise it would be given. She checked for soundness and strength, feeling through her hands, using instinct and knowledge. She kept detailed records of each animal's daily performance.

As she inspected each horse, she gave precise instructions to the person who exercised that horse. She wanted no misunderstandings, no mistakes. Each horse was valuable. Never was she more conscious of their value than during the morning workout, when their energy made them jumpy and nervous.

She mounted Shay's Pride just as the sun peeked over the horizon, heralding another hot summer day. The dark sky edged toward crystal blue clarity. No cloud marred the perfect opalescence. The sprinklers went on, misting the air.

Shay's Pride pranced sideways, shaking his head nervously. Liz nudged his sides with her heels and he jumped forward, almost unseating her.

"He looks temperamental today." Chance leaned against the fence, looking as tired as Liz. He wore jeans with a white shirt and a silk scarf knotted about his throat. A wide-brimmed Stetson shaded his eyes.

"Must have had a bad night." Liz tried to relax, to feel the animal under her. Part of her success with horses

118   *That Winning Touch*

was her ability to intuit their feelings. She didn't like the way Shay's Pride moved.

She nodded at Allen, who started Ayala through her warmup. Andrea followed on Silverado. Kippy rode Betsy Ross. The animals looked beautiful with the sunlight bouncing off their glossy coats and eyes alive with excitement.

"Soon," Liz whispered to Shay's Pride, feeling his tense muscles bunch under her. She wanted to calm the animal, but he continued to toss his head fitfully, snorting and shying, playing against the bit with his tongue.

As each horse sped around the track, Liz recorded its performance in the small notebook she kept in her shirt pocket. She couldn't concentrate this morning, the lack of sleep leaving her numb and lethargic. With Chance watching so closely, she was caught between intense awareness of him and the agitated horse under her. She was unable to focus on either.

Finally, she released Shay's Pride. She felt his powerful muscles move into the first part of his warm-up. In the next instant, she found herself on the ground staring up at the sky. Above her, she watched the rising hooves of the horse. As the mighty hooves started down, she rolled away, distantly hearing shouts and cries.

Stunned, she lay in the dirt. Dust clogged her nose. She coughed. Her chest hurt. She couldn't seem to breathe. Chance turned her over. He spoke, but she couldn't hear. Beyond him, she saw Kippy reaching for Shay's Pride, grasping the reins firmly and wrapping an arm around the frightened animal's neck.

"What happened?" She found her voice.

"Lie still." Chance pushed her flat on the ground.

That Winning Touch   119

"Andrea, tell Margie to phone Dr. Jordan. Tell her Liz has been thrown and is in shock."

"I'm fine." The shock began to wear off, and Liz felt a thread of pain. She'd been thrown before. She wasn't hurt. Was she? Darkness seeped along the edge of her vision. With a sigh, she stopped struggling and fell back, unconscious.

"How is she?" Liz heard a distant voice and struggled to open her eyes. She was able to open them to slits and found herself lying in a hospital room.

"She's going to be just fine," a brisk voice answered. A woman came into view, her gray hair knotted at the back of her head and a stethoscope dangling from her neck. "Hello, there." The woman bent over Liz and gently flashed a light in her eyes. "I'm Dr. Jordan. You've taken a nasty tumble. How do you feel?"

"Groggy." Liz tried to assess the damage, but couldn't feel anything. A shape flashed across the edge of her vision and she saw Dicey sitting on a stool in the corner. She smiled and wriggled her fingers at Liz.

"You've got a mild concussion and a broken wrist, I'm afraid." Dr. Jordan listened to Liz's lungs. "All clear. And your heart is pumping along just fine. I'd say you're as healthy as a horse, or maybe I should compare you to something else." The doctor chuckled as she continued her examination.

Liz raised her hands. One arm was so heavy, she could barely lift it. Her wrist was encased in a cast. As she examined the plaster, a dull, throbbing ache coursed up her arm.

The door to the examining room opened and Chance

walked in. He approached the bed and smiled at her. "How are you feeling?"

"I don't know yet," she said.

Dr. Jordan stepped back. "She's fine. A bit shaken, with a mild concussion and broken wrist." Dr. Jordan sat down on a stool. She wrote as she spoke. "I'm going to prescribe a mild painkiller. I suggest you go home and sleep. You'll feel better tomorrow."

"And the concussion?" Chance asked.

Liz struggled to sit up and he helped her, supporting her as gently as he could. The room swam for a minute before righting itself. Liz saw Andrea, her face white and frightened. Liz offered her a tremulous smile, but the girl didn't return it.

Dr. Jordan handed Chance a prescription form. "Don't worry about the concussion. Just take her home, put her to bed, and wake her every once in a while."

A large clock on the wall clicked as the second hand whirled around its face. Eight o'clock. Had she lost two hours or fourteen? She sat on the edge of the bed. Andrea edged close and slid a hand inside hers. Liz squeezed and tried to give a reassuring smile, but Andrea didn't look reassured.

Dr. Jordan handed the chart to Chance. "You can take her home, if you'll just sign here." He signed where she pointed.

"Thanks, Dr. Jordan," he said.

She nodded. "A nurse will be along in a second with a wheelchair."

"I can walk." Liz slid down to the floor, but the floor started to weave and move.

Chance grabbed her. "We'll wait for the wheelchair."

Dr. Jordan said, "The nurse will bring a sling for that

That Winning Touch   121

wrist. Keep your arm still for a few days. The throbbing will go away. I want to see you in my office in three days.'' She left abruptly without another word.

Dicey rested a hand on Liz's shoulder, looking as shaken and pale as Andrea. The nurse arrived with the wheelchair and sling, and in a few more minutes, Liz was helped into the Mercedes.

''We'll have you home in no time.'' Chance drove out of the hospital parking lot.

''What about Shay's Pride?'' she asked.

''He's fine. Don't worry. Sam and Allen went over him very carefully.''

Liz rested her head against the headrest. The throbbing in her wrist lessened. She started to feel normal again except for her extreme exhaustion.

She slept the rest of the morning. When she woke, the house was deserted except for Dicey, who sat in the living room reading the newspaper.

''Should you be out of bed?'' Dicey jumped to her feet when she entered.

''I'm fine.'' Liz sat down gingerly on the sofa and swung her feet onto the cushions. She eased her wrist across her stomach and slid down until her head lay against the armrest. ''Where is everyone?''

''At the fair.'' Dicey set aside the newspaper. ''Chance took Andrea to her competition, and Margie and the guests went along.''

''I promised I'd go too.'' Liz shifted until she felt comfortable. Her head seemed clearer, but her wrist ached. She should check Shay's Pride, but she couldn't force herself up.

''Andrea's not upset. She said she'd win first place just for you. So be proud of her when she gets back.''

122   *That Winning Touch*

"You know so much about being a mother."

"I think about it." Dicey laughed. "But then I think about Susanna Brentwood and how she abandoned Andrea."

Liz bunched a cushion behind her neck and sighed as she relaxed. The sofa was more comfortable than her bed. "Do you know Susanna?"

Dicey took a long, deep breath. "Yes. She's the most useless person I know. She's more useless than I am. She's wrecked her life and her daughter's, and missed the best years of Andrea's childhood. I'm no gem, but I didn't abandon my baby to be raised by an uncle."

"What about the father?" Liz asked, a little abashed at her curiosity.

"Mitch Brentwood!" Dicey laughed. "A mongrel if there ever was one. I thought I loved him once." She drew back into silence, a look of pain in her eyes, then shrugged. "He married Susanna instead."

"I don't think you're useless, Dicey." Liz closed her eyes. "Just misdirected. You need something to do with your life."

A knock sounded on the back door. Dicey jumped to her feet, a look of relief on her face as she ran to answer it. Liz heard voices and then she returned, followed by Allen.

He held a saddle under his arm, the girth draped over his wrist. "Hi, Liz."

Liz sat up, suddenly alert, her painful wrist forgotten. "Is something wrong, Allen?"

He stood silently in front of her and handed her the broken end of the girth. Liz squinted at it. The strap of leather looked as if the edges had been neatly sliced except for a jagged corner. Someone had cut the leather, leaving

That Winning Touch   123

just enough to hold it together until it separated naturally. She touched the smooth cut. What did this mean?

"I didn't discover it until after all the excitement when I was unsaddling Shay's Pride," Allen said.

"Who saddled him?" Liz asked.

"I did." He looked pained. "I swear to you nothing was wrong with that girth when I first saddled the horse."

She laid a hand on his arm. "I believe you."

Dicey leaned over the arm of the sofa and stared intently at the girth. "Are you saying someone tried to kill you?"

"I think this was meant more to scare me than anything else." What was going on here? Liz wondered. Chance had some fine thoroughbreds with outstanding pedigrees that weren't performing as they should. Now, someone seemed determined to keep her from finding out why.

"You should tell Chance," Dicey said.

"I will."

A few minutes after Allen left, Chance and Andrea returned.

"Look!" Andrea held her blue ribbon aloft for Liz to see. "I won showmanship, first place." She grinned. "And Sir Lancealop won Best of Show!" She did a happy jig around the room.

"Congratulations." Liz smiled to see Andrea so happy. Chance beamed with pride as he watched his niece.

"How do you feel?" Chance asked, leaning over her.

"Embarrassed at being tossed so easily. I've been riding friskier horses than Shay's Pride all my life," she replied. She would tell Chance about the cut saddle girth later, not in front of Andrea.

124   *That Winning Touch*

Margie entered, a tray in her hands. "You certainly provided us with a morning full of excitement."

Chance sat down with his legs extended and eyes half closed. He watched Liz with such intensity, she could feel the telltale heat of embarrassment creeping up her face. What was he thinking about? Last night and their walk on the beach? Or something else?

Andrea chattered, reliving her moment of glory. Liz found herself drifting off to sleep. Her wrist throbbed. Not until Chance suddenly scooped her up in his arms and took her to her room did she realize how much she wanted the unconsciousness the painkillers would give her.

The Fourth of July dawned clear and sunny. Liz spent the morning watching the horses. Although the pain in her wrist had abated somewhat, she was still conscious of the heaviness of the cast and the deep bone-throbbing ache.

After the workout, she sat in her office listening to the restless movements of the horses in the stalls. Outside, the occasional crack of fireworks kept the nervous horses from settling down to a restful calm.

She looked up just as Dicey walked in. "Are you coming to the picnic this afternoon?" Dicey asked.

"I don't know. Chance's clients make me uncomfortable." She'd already seen a well-known actress and her husband and knew the woman was Chance's client.

"Come anyway." Dicey blushed like a young girl. "I'd like you to get to know Paul. He's really a nice man."

Liz thought he was the only real man Dicey had ever known, considering her beach-bum tastes. Dicey was en-

That Winning Touch 125

titled to more. Liz didn't understand why Dicey chose such unsuitable men. Paul was so different. She yawned.

"Didn't you sleep well last night?" Dicey asked in a solicitous tone.

Lethargically, Liz rubbed her arms. "No." She'd awakened early to get a drink of water and then had sat for an hour looking out the window at the hushed barn area, thinking about Chance.

"You'll feel better soon. Got to go—it's time to start getting ready for the picnic." She walked out to the gravel path and waved.

Liz drew the accounting books to her. At her elbow, a pile of VCR tape cassettes shifted. She restacked them. The tapes held recordings of every race Chance's horses had been in. She'd started studying them, using his office when possible, or the television in her room. She'd been trying to understand why Silverado's early performances on the track had been so erratic, and why the rest of Chance's horses had suddenly stopped winning, except for an occasional showing in second or third place.

She finished some paperwork. Rubbing the back of her neck, she stood up. Slowly, she became aware of voices arguing. She paused, her head tilted toward the heating duct over her head. She stepped closer, trying to make out the angry words. Curious, she left her office and walked around the edge of the stable and into the feed alley.

The alley was empty except for Betsy Ross, cross-tied between two beams.

Liz approached the stall. Allen stood inside raking the bedding.

"Hi." He shoveled the soiled straw into a wheelbarrow.

126   *That Winning Touch*

"I heard two people arguing," Liz said.

"Nobody here but me," he said, stepping out and looking up and down. "Though Sam was here a few seconds ago."

"Anyone with him?"

Allen shook his head, his eyes puzzled. "I didn't see anyone. Did you hear what the argument was about?"

Liz opened the doors on either side of Betsy Ross's stall. One was empty; the other contained Silverado, scratching his rump against the manger.

"I couldn't hear clearly." She hooked the upper door shut and glanced at Allen. He shrugged.

She walked down the alley, then paused to listen. The voices had come from too far away. She walked back.

Allen returned Betsy Ross to her stall. "Find anything?"

"No." She passed him and walked out into the morning heat. Shrill laughter reached her. She found Chance standing in her office, a woman hanging on to his arms. The woman glanced at Liz, dismissal in her eyes.

Chance shook the woman free, a look of relief in his eyes. "Liz, I've been looking for you."

The woman grinned brightly. When she tried to take Chance's hand, he eluded her, stepping up to Liz and hooking his arm through hers. His touch brought back memories of their walk on the beach. She felt heat flame within her.

"So that's the way it goes," the woman said. She turned on her heel and left without a backward glance.

"I didn't think I'd get rid of her." His arm tightened around Liz. "How are you feeling? You still look tired."

She wondered how she'd managed to resist him so long. Despite the awkwardness she felt, she managed a

That Winning Touch 127

calm smile. "My wrist ached all night, but it's less painful today. While you slept this morning, I got up and exercised your animals."

He chuckled. A frantic, half-formed recklessness took hold of Liz. He touched her chin, his fingers giving a light, feathery caress.

Sam gave a little cough. "Excuse me."

Liz broke away, a warm blush on her cheeks. Sam's eyes mocked her.

"What is it, Sam?" Chance said.

She forced her mind into composure, her gaze resting on Sam, wondering what he had on his mind. She glanced at her watch. Usually he had left for lunch by now.

"Didn't mean to interrupt," Sam said smoothly. His eyes betrayed contempt as he watched Liz. "What time is the picnic? I need to ready the horses."

"I told you, one o'clock." Chance sounded annoyed. "Why ask again?"

"Just checking. The pickup is loaded. Once you and your guests leave, I'll drive to the picnic area and start the barbecues." He turned on his heel and left. The gravel scrunched under his feet as he headed down the path toward the garage.

"Sorry for the interruption." Chance took her hands.

"What horses are you planning to use?" Liz asked.

"All the neighbor kids' animals, plus Divinity Fudge for you. She's pretty easy to handle since I retired her from the track. Despite a broken wrist, I know you won't be satisfied on anything less than a thoroughbred. Or would you prefer to ride in the truck with Sam?"

Liz vehemently shook her head no.

Chance laughed. "I didn't think so. I'm riding Deadly Justice, since you aren't taking him to Del Mar."

128   *That Winning Touch*

"I didn't know I was invited to the picnic." She scooped up the videotapes from the desk. "I planned to study these tapes."

"This is the Fourth of July—a holiday, Liz." A mischievous grin gave him a boyish look. "You're not working today. You're going to play a little."

"Your friends make me uncomfortable." She hugged the tapes to her chest. She drew in ragged breaths, still unrecovered from the power of her feelings for Chance. When did people know they were in love? She thought she had known with Timmy, but these feelings were so different. Nothing so wonderful had ever happened to her before.

Chance took the tapes out of her arms and restacked them on the desk. "You'll like my friends. Most of them are clients, and quite nice. Even in the entertainment industry, people are people. They will all be leaving first thing in the morning, and we'll still have the weekend just for us."

His eyes offered a promise that made her weak at the knees. "What do you have planned for the weekend?" she asked.

"We could go to the zoo. Or one last jaunt to the fair, or a trip to Mexico? Have you ever been to Tijuana? I know this restaurant in the hills that serves the best roasted goat and handmade tortillas. Have you ever had goat meat?"

"No. I've always heard the food in Mexico is a gamble." She'd gone to Aqua Caliente, the racetrack in Tijuana, but the broken-down hacks on the track had saddened her. The horses had been unfit to race, and Liz had felt sorry for them. The thoroughbreds had not looked

That Winning Touch   **129**

particularly mistreated, but neither had they looked healthy.

"The food from the street vendors should be avoided, but not the more reputable restaurants."

"I'll have to think about Mexico," Liz said as she approached the house. With her morning chores completed, she had a few minutes to rest. She intended to take advantage of the time.

A friend of Chance's hailed him from the pool area. He turned away from Liz to fulfill his duties as host.

A glow illuminated Liz's soul. She lay in the shade of a lacy pepper tree, listening to the lethargic drone of insects. The jingle of a horse's bridle punctuated the cry of a golden eagle soaring overhead. An occasional car drove down the lane bordering the state park picnic area.

"Sleeping?" Chance sat down next to her on the blanket.

Lazily, she opened her eyes, unable to remember ever feeling so tired yet so alive. Being near Chance led her thoughts off into dangerous directions, despite the fear in the back of her mind reminding her that everything ended—even love.

"Being lazy." She ran fingers through her hair. Distantly she heard Dicey laugh, then silence, then more laughter.

"Still want to be lazy?" he asked, the tone of his voice dangerously seductive as he tickled her ribs.

Laughing, she slid away from him. He held on to her hand, preventing her from going too far. His laughter joined in hers.

A shadow fell over them. Sam stood in front of them, his mouth twisted into a broken line, anger darkening his

130   *That Winning Touch*

eyes. When Chance looked up, Sam's face cleared and
he smiled.

"Sky's clouding up." Sam gestured at the sky. "Radio
says rain. It's time we got these tenderfeet back home."

Chance jumped up. He caught himself on the trunk of
the tree when his leg buckled. "Let's round up everybody. It's a good hour's ride back."

Liz helped steady him. Then she folded the blanket,
draping it over her arm. Chance walked away, calling
for his guests.

"Think you're mighty smart, don't you?" Sam caught
hold of her before she could follow Chance. "Snugglin'
up with Chance. I know what you're doing."

"Let go." Liz pulled out of his grip.

"In the end, he'll believe me before he believes you."
He gave her a crooked smile.

"About what?" She studied him. His smile broadened.
He winked at her and walked away before she could react.

Liz stood rooted to the spot. A chill moved over her.
What was Sam talking about? What did he mean?

Chance's guests moved reluctantly back toward the
horses. A cold, brisk wind sprang up, lifting Liz's curls,
ruffling them about her face. She could almost smell the
coming rain, even though the sun still shone brightly.
Trails of clouds moved across the sky. She shivered.
Chance waved to her. She started toward him, felt someone watching her, and stopped.

Sam leaned against the fender of the truck, a cigarette
dangling from his lips. He smiled, then climbed inside
the cab.

She handed the blanket to Chance. "Why don't you
wrap this around Dicey? She's looking a little cold."

Mounted on a long-legged gelding, Dicey rubbed her

That Winning Touch 131

arms. The temperature had fallen a few degrees. The wind grew colder.

"Let's get home before the rain starts." Chance swung aboard his horse. "Let's go." He turned toward the lane.

Andrea and Pete took the middle and Liz brought up the rear, helping those who didn't know how to ride too well. They rode back to the ranch as quickly as possible. The guests dismounted. Liz, Andrea, and Pete led the animals to the stables to be cooled down and then fed.

As she rubbed down her horse, Liz couldn't help thinking about Sam's words. She shivered from the chill that suddenly swept over her.

Chapter Eight

"ARE you busy?" Andrea entered Chance's office, looking very pretty in white shorts and a blue shirt. Her blond hair, drawn back from her face, revealed soft, childlike curves slowly maturing into the angular structure of a woman.

"Come in." Chance was startled at her appearance. Each year he watched her grow to look more like her mother. He could only hope that Andrea did not share Susanna's problems.

"Can I talk to you?" Andrea perched on the edge of a chair, looking tense and miserable.

He closed the book he'd been reading. He leaned back expectantly. He realized he hadn't spent much time with her and he felt a bit guilty.

"What's on your mind, pumpkin?" His old endearment for her hung in the air between them. She looked startled.

"Do you like Liz?" she asked with a sideways glance at him.

He felt a little uncomfortable discussing Liz with Andrea, but she did have the right to know that he'd found someone he liked enough to contemplate a long-term relationship.

132

That Winning Touch 133

"Are you going to marry her?" she continued bluntly, fiddling with the ends of her hair.

He owed her an honest answer. "I don't think Liz is ready for marriage." Nor would she give up her career easily. Racing was a part of her. She would have problems giving up the vagabond life she so enjoyed for something more stable.

"I really like her," Andrea continued, her eyes going dark and slightly wary. "I don't want you to hurt her feelings."

"I won't, honey," Chance assured her.

"I heard Sam saying rotten things about her to you yesterday. You listened to him. Did you believe him?" She grew more tense, more rigid, her chin thrust forward.

"Sam's upset," Chance said. "He feels the trainer's job belongs to him." He worried a little over Sam's obsession with Liz. Chance tried to be patient, tried to understand. Sam had given his life to Brentwood Farms.

"Why do you like Sam so much?"

"He's my friend." Chance wondered why Andrea was questioning him about it. Sam had been like a father to her, had loved her almost as much as his own son. "I've known Sam all my life. He's loyal to me. I owe him the same loyalty in return."

Andrea frowned. "I don't like him. And I hate Jack. He scares me."

Chance began to feel a trickle of alarm. Andrea had never been so insistent before. "Jack has a few problems. But you know Sam would never let anything happen to you."

"He didn't do anything when Jack hid around corners and tried to scare me. I told Sam and asked him to make Jack stop, but Sam laughed at me."

134 *That Winning Touch*

Chance suddenly sat up straight. He gazed sharply at Andrea. Her shadowed eyes hinted at long-held anger. "Why didn't you tell me this before?"

"I did, but you wouldn't listen." The set of her mouth tightened. "Sam told you Jack was just playing games. You believed him and not me. Now you'll believe him about Liz, and you'll get rid of Liz because Sam doesn't like her."

Chance worried at the truth in her words. "Did Jack ever hurt you?" he asked, wondering why he'd taken Sam's word over Andrea's. She shook her head sadly, and he continued, "Don't worry, pumpkin. I won't let anything happen to you—or to Liz."

Andrea looked at him with doubt in her eyes. "Don't believe Sam when he says bad things about Liz. And don't let Jack come back!" She jumped up, her hair swinging forward with the force of her action. Her mouth opened, then snapped shut.

"Andrea, what's worrying you?" Chance said, reaching out to her. But she slipped from his grasp and left without answering. He tried to run after her, but she'd already fled down the hall and out the back door.

Mulling over his niece's words, Chance worried that Sam hadn't been as truthful with him as he had been with Sam.

Over the next weeks, Chance watched the frenetic energy of the stables grow even more frantic. Liz became short-tempered and irritable. She spent her nights watching videos of all the races his horses had run, making notes, and discussing strategy with Sam and Allen. Sam unbent enough to offer advice, but Chance had no idea if she used his comments.

That Winning Touch 135

Chance cut down on the time he spent in Los Angeles, turning over the major part of his work to his partners. He wanted to be near Liz, watching her work. Sitting in his office day after day, he stared out the window at the stables. Even the horses seemed to know what was happening around them. Silverado had a tantrum that nearly rebroke Liz's wrist. Betsy Ross, always serene and calm, tried to kick down her stall door. The other horses walked around the yard as if treading on eggshells.

"You've really got it bad for that broad, don't you?" Sam drew Chance's attention from the window one day.

Chance looked at the door. He admired Sam, but lately he felt impatience for the man. "I didn't hear you knock, Sam."

"You want me to go back and do it again?" Sam settled his thin, wiry figure into a chair and stared at him. "The little girly really has your mind in a whirl."

"She's a woman." He swiveled back to the window. A truck loaded with hay pulled up to the side of the feed barn. Liz handed two curving hay hooks to Allen. Since she couldn't help unload because of her wrist, she stood to one side and directed. Allen helped the driver unload, hauling hundred-pound bales of hay, tossing them around as if they weighed nothing.

Chance swiveled back to face Sam. "Do you have something to say?" he asked.

Sam's eyes narrowed. "What's she saying about me? Nothin' good, I guess." He grinned, showing teeth stained yellow. He smelled sharply of whiskey. He prepared to spit a stream of tobacco juice, changed his mind and swallowed the juice with a grimace. "Get rid of her before there's trouble."

"Trouble from you?" Chance's eyebrows arched.

136   *That Winning Touch*

"She's tearin' us apart. We used to be friends, Chance. I taught you to ride. Your daddy assured me I'd have a home here all my life." A plaintive whine invaded his voice. "It hasn't felt much like a home lately, what with her giving me orders."

Chance wondered where the conversation was going. Sam had something in mind, but what? "Liz knows racing," he said. "The horses have never looked better. I feel this is going to be a winning season for us." Next week—Del Mar.

"She fired my boy. I want him back," Sam said, his voice agitated. "I haven't heard from him since he left. That girly destroyed my boy, and now she's destroying me." He slumped, his face crumpled with a father's grief. He wiped his eyes with the back of his hand.

"You and I both know Jack stayed here because he got free rent. It's about time he grew up and found out that life consists of more than a minimum of work." Chance was glad Jack had left. He'd whined that his life wasn't as privileged as Chance's, that he deserved better. "Let him go. Let him find his own way. He's not a child anymore."

Sam got to his feet, looking old and tired. "I thought you were my friend." He shuffled out the door, snapping it closed.

Chance sat back. He'd always felt loyal to Sam, but even his loyalty had its limits. He remembered what Andrea had said about Jack and how Sam had twisted her complaints. He began to doubt that Sam was the good family friend he claimed to be.

Liz walked through the feed barn. Three hundred bales of hay and bedding straw and a hundred sacks of feed

That Winning Touch 137

had been neatly stacked against the wall. The grain bins were full. She had enough feed for all the animals on the property for at least two months. She would have ordered more hay, but the feed barn wasn't big enough, and she wouldn't stack the bales outside where the humid night air would cause them to rot.

In her office, she found Andrea sitting on the edge of her desk. Since the end of the fair, the girl had been moody. Her rabbits had done extremely well and Liz had hung all the blue ribbons on the office wall, where everyone could see them. Although Andrea seemed to have pride in her achievements, her mood grew steadily worse.

"What's wrong, Andrea?" Liz tried to be patient. She remembered her awkward preteen years and feelings of rejection.

"My uncle," Andrea said, a woebegone cast to her face.

"Don't complain to me," Liz said in a reasonable tone. "Complain to him." Whatever problems Andrea felt she had, she had to solve them herself. Liz couldn't interfere.

"He doesn't listen to me." Andrea bit the ends of her hair, holding the strands between her teeth and staring pensively at Liz. "I tried to tell him how I feel, but he didn't understand."

Outside, Liz watched Barbie guide her mare across the grass, the foal following right behind. The afternoon sun cast long shadows on the ground. The pepper tree shading her office swayed in the ocean breeze.

"You haven't given him much opportunity. All you do is snarl at him."

"He won't listen to me," Andrea insisted.

"I've heard this before. What I see doesn't match what you tell me. He loves you. I don't understand why you

138 *That Winning Touch*

insist he doesn't. He took you to the fair and watched your competition and was terribly proud of you.''

She sensed that Andrea was using Chance's lack of love as an excuse for something else that bothered her. But what? The girl looked lost and afraid. Liz wanted to take her in her arms and soothe away her sadness, but she didn't know how to make the first move. She tried to think. Her wrist ached slightly. The heavy cast had been replaced by a light plastic one secured to her wrist with straps.

A shadow darkened the door. The blacksmith walked in, touching the brim of his San Diego Padres baseball cap. ''Miss Stratton, I shoed all the horses except Silverado. I was just wondering if you want his regular plates on, or the other ones?''

Liz stood up, suddenly alert. ''What other ones?''

Andrea slid past the blacksmith and ran across the lawn to Barbie, still walking her horse.

''You know. . . .'' The man looked uncomfortable. He brushed his hands across his leather apron.

''Show me what you're talking about.''

She followed him to his trailer, which he'd set up on the grass. The back stood open. He handed two shoe plates to her.

''What is this?'' She turned the shoes over, staring at the uneven line. She'd never seen a pair of racing shoes like this before. They felt too heavy to be aluminum, yet their outer casing appeared to be just that. Each plate had a brace across the center and a thickness around the edges that was greater than normal. ''What faults do these shoes correct?'' she asked.

''It's Sam's design,'' the blacksmith said. ''He told me they help a horse race better.''

That Winning Touch 139

Liz hefted the shoes. The weight was distributed so unevenly, she doubted a horse could walk properly in them. No wonder Deadly Justice had sore feet if the blacksmith had been using shoes like this on him. "Do you do blacksmithing for other racing stables?"

"No, ma'am. My other clients are pleasure horses." He looked upset as he reached out to take the plates, but Liz held on.

"I'll keep these." She hefted them again, feeling the imbalance. "Put regular racing plates on Silverado." She turned and ran toward the house, bursting into Chance's office and tossing the plates on his desk. They thudded heavily. "Look at this."

"They're horseshoes," Chance replied, puzzled.

"Not on any horse I've ever run." Liz picked up a plate and turned it over and over, measuring the unevenness in form and weight. "The blacksmith tells me Sam designed these shoes."

"Sam knows what he's doing."

Bitterly, Liz replied, "I'm certain he does. Hold the other one. Do you feel the irregular distribution of weight? I've never seen anything like this before."

Chance turned the plate around. "I don't know what you're getting at."

"I did some checking on Silverado's past wins and losses. I called the tracks where he raced and talked to the track managers. They say your horses are just as likely to win as lose, and no one seems able to predict what they'll do. Does that suggest anything to you?" She watched Chance turn the shoes over in his hand.

"Are you saying the horses are somehow programmed to lose?"

Liz was worried. Had Sam been cheating Chance for

140 *That Winning Touch*

years? She tapped the heel of one of the shoes. ''I think Silverado and your other animals wear this type of shoe when they aren't supposed to win, and a regular racing plate when they are. If an animal loses enough, the track recorder puts him down in class and no one bets. Then suddenly, after six, seven, eight losses, your horse wins. The track checks for drugs in the system, but no one ever looks at a horse's feet.''

''What is this designed to do?'' Chance stared at the gleaming metal plate.

''I think a shoe like this would put a horse off its stride just enough to keep it from doing its best.'' She felt a little sick as she watched the changing emotions cross Chance's face.

''But why?'' His jaw tightened, and his eyes turned dark with suspicion.

''I don't know.'' Why would anyone want a horse to lose? Because they wanted another horse to win? Liz tried to clear her thoughts. A program of unpredictable wins seemed too risky. But if a horse was supposed to lose a race. . . .

Chance opened a drawer and put the shoes inside. ''I'll ask Sam. I'm sure he has a reasonable explanation.''

''I'm sure he does. I'd like to hear it too.'' She wondered what Sam would say to get out of this.

''I'll talk to Sam alone, thank you.'' Chance used the edge of the desk to lever himself to his feet. He grabbed his cane and stalked around Liz.

''Now?'' she asked.

''Later, after dinner. Wait for me in the Jacuzzi and I'll join you after my talk with him.''

Liz watched him leave. Somehow, she didn't think he would get the right answers. He liked racing, but didn't

That Winning Touch 141

know much about the logistics of the sport. Sam had just enough knowledge to form a logical answer that sounded good, but it wouldn't be the right one. Whatever Sam was up to, Chance was unlikely to find out.

After dinner, when the sun had gone down and the intolerable heat had abated, Liz changed into her swimsuit and spent a long time soaking in the Jacuzzi. She leaned against the lip, her body almost floating. She wondered what was happening in Chance's office. He didn't come. Worried, she stared at the lights outlining his window.

The patio lights cast shadows along the edges of the walk. In the next instant, they went out. Liz thought someone from the house had switched the lights off. She hooked her elbow over the lip of the Jacuzzi, preparing to haul herself out of the water.

She heard footsteps on the concrete pad. "Chance?" Then someone grabbed her, pushing her under the water.

Liz flailed, trying to grasp the edge and pull herself up, but she slipped on the plastic bottom of the Jacuzzi. The hand held her under until she saw spots in front of her eyes. Little by little, dark edges clouded her mind. She clutched at the hand holding her under, and felt gloves and a long-sleeved shirt.

Her strength ebbed. She tried to look up, but the darkness concealed her attacker. She sank toward the bottom. Her body went limp. She floated downward, dreamily thinking how easy it would be to let go and stay at the bottom of the Jacuzzi. . . .

Liz regained consciousness slowly. She coughed and sputtered. Bitter water spurted out of her mouth. She coughed again, harder.

142   *That Winning Touch*

Someone bent over her, holding her tightly. She screamed.

"Open your eyes, you're all right," Chance cried. He shook her. "I told you never to sit in the Jacuzzi by yourself. You get so comfortable in the hot water, your whole body relaxes and you slide underwater without being aware."

Tears slid out of the corners of her eyes. She wasn't dead. She pushed him away weakly. The pool area was lit again.

"Someone tried to kill me." Hysteria rose in her. The taste of chlorine filled her mouth. "Sam tried to kill me."

He sat back on his heels. "Hardly," he said in a cold tone. "Sam's been with me in my office all evening. He just left, and I came down here and found you on the bottom."

Liz rolled to her feet. She staggered.

Chance caught her. "You must have hit your head. You're not making any sense."

Sam wouldn't be stupid enough to try to harm her. Who, then? Jack?

Her tongue tasted of chlorine. "I was waiting for you. Then the pool lights went out. Someone grabbed me and pushed me under. I couldn't twist away." Frightened, she clung to him.

"The lights were on when I came out." He slid an arm around her and guided her along the path that led to her bedroom. "Let's get you to bed. You seem to be confused."

Stubbornly, Liz started to repeat her accusation, but the stern look on Chance's face stopped her. She closed her eyes, but the darkness behind her lids brought reminders of the attack.

That Winning Touch 143

Someone had tried to hurt her. Did her attacker want to kill her or just frighten her? If someone had wanted her dead, there was plenty of opportunity. All the attacker had to do was leave the pool lights off. Chance would not have looked for her there. He'd have gone to her room and then searched the house first. By that time, she'd have been long dead. She shivered.

Once in the house, she noticed Chance was tense. He glanced back at the pool area.

"What's wrong?" she asked softly. A silvery moon lit the open window. The curtains stirred slightly in the light breeze. She could hear the rustle of the wind through the leaves of the pepper trees surrounding the house.

"I don't know." He turned back to her. "We've had too many accidents to be a coincidence."

Liz went into the bathroom and talked through the door as she stripped her suit off and dressed in work clothes. Her jeans smelled of horse sweat and saddle leather and reminded her of her father after a long day at the track.

"I wish I knew." She came out and sat down on a sofa, and Chance sat next to her.

He moved restlessly while she gazed at his profile. She didn't feel fear, she felt anger. Whoever wanted to hurt her had not only attacked her in the Jacuzzi but had cut the girth under Shay's Pride's saddle. But she wouldn't be frightened off by two halfhearted attacks. She'd faced stiffer adversity than this.

Chance's arms slipped around her. She leaned into the embrace, eyes closed. She felt womanly and attractive.

Liz had spent years trying to make the racing world accept her not as her father's daughter but as herself. Sometimes, she forgot about the feminine side of her

144   *That Winning Touch*

nature. She needed to be tough to survive. Had she grown
too tough?

"What did Sam say about the special shoes he designed
for Silverado?" she finally asked.

He'd known she would ask and dreaded the question.
He'd been so happy that morning. What had happened
to destroy his feelings of contentment?

When he didn't answer, she repeated her question.

He caught her hand in his, feeling the ridge of calluses
on the inside of her palm. "The shoes are to correct a
fault in Silverado's feet. The horse runs better with
them." Even to his own ears, he sounded unconvinced,
the explanation hollow.

Sam was a lifelong friend. How could he not believe
him? Yet a niggling doubt surfaced. He pushed the whisper away.

"And you believed him." She sounded resigned.

"I've known Sam all my life, and I've known you
only a few weeks." He didn't know whom to believe.
Sam? Liz? Not even Andrea had good things to say about
Sam or Jack. But what about Liz? He'd hired her to do
a job, and then he'd put obstacles in her way.

A chasm seemed to open. She put inches between them
that felt like miles. "I've spent my whole life following
the racing circuit. Never before have I seen racing shoes
like the ones Sam claims help a horse do better on the
track."

He felt her withdrawing from him. "Sam knows racing
too."

"Don't you trust me?" She moved to the edge of the
sofa, the distance between them growing.

In his mind, Chance suddenly heard his brother asking
him the same thing: *Don't you trust me?* Mitch had said

That Winning Touch 145

when Chance had confronted him with his out-of-control gambling, the wreck of his marriage, and Andrea caught in the tug-of-war between two unfeeling parents.

Stiffly, Liz stood up and faced him. Even in the moonlight, he could see the set lines of her face, the coldness in her eyes. Suddenly, he didn't know whom to trust anymore.

"You don't believe me when I say someone tried to harm me tonight?" Her voice echoed across the room. "Maybe not to kill me, but to frighten me. Don't you think it's a little too accidental to happen just after I discovered Sam's fancy racing shoes? You say Sam was with you, but what about Jack?"

"Jack's in New York." Chance wanted to believe her, but who else harbored such angry feelings against her aside from Sam and his son? Both could account for their whereabouts.

Shaken, Liz sat down again. "Jack's in New York?" Doubt reflected in her eyes. Chance wanted to touch her, to draw her into his arms, but the stiffness in her body stopped him.

"He left the day you fired him. He's been in New York ever since." Chance sat up, knowing she'd ask him to leave now.

"Someone really did try to frighten me." Her voice rippled with fear. She reached out to him, but her feathery touches on his arm did nothing to bridge the gap growing between them.

He heard the plaintive note in her tone, asking him to believe her. He did. Yet Sam was his friend and he couldn't dismiss her accusations against him so easily.

"I'll see you in the morning." Chance leaned over and kissed her cheek. She trembled. "I'm sorry."

146 *That Winning Touch*

He turned at the door to look at her. She sat on the sofa, arms clasped around her knees, her eyes haunted holes of misery.

"Are we going back to a business relationship?" She sounded bitter. Chance didn't blame her. He'd hurt her, even after he'd promised her he wouldn't.

"I need to go to Los Angeles for a few days. We'll discuss it when I return." He left, closing the door and leaning against it. He thought he heard a gulping sob, but only silence greeted him when he pressed his ear to the door. He needed to be away from her, to recover his emotional balance.

He heard another door shut, but when he looked down the hall, he saw nothing but a long line of closed doors.

He limped back to his room. If he didn't find a way to solve the dilemma, he'd lose Liz. And nothing would ever make up for her loss.

He lay in bed all night staring at the ceiling, until the early-morning light crept through the window. Then he got up, showered, and packed. Long before anyone missed him, he'd be in Los Angeles.

Chapter Nine

Racing day dawned clear and breezy with a huge yellow sun beating down on the track. Ocean winds kept the grounds cool. Liz leaned over the door to a stall, smiling at Silverado, who paced back and forth, tail held high, feet rustling the straw. He lifted his head to sniff the air, nostrils extended, neck arched.

"He looks good," Chance said, coming to stand near Liz.

Deep in her contemplation, she hadn't heard him approach. With eyes hooded and black hair tousled by the wind, he looked tired.

She hadn't expected him to come to the track. She brushed her palms on the seat of her jeans and held out grimy fingers to him. "Hello, Chance." She congratulated herself on the cool tone of her voice. Nothing gave away the turbulence of her heart and soul at seeing him again.

Moving aside, she tried to ignore the ache in her heart. He'd been gone a week, and he looked as awful as she felt. Black circles ringed his eyes. His mouth held a cynical twist she hadn't noticed before. Seeing him again brought memories of late-night swims, a walk on the beach, a day at the fair, and a picnic at the state park.

147

They'd had so few precious weeks of being in love. Again a man had deceived her.

"He's in the best condition he's ever been in." Liz couldn't help the pride in her voice. Yet as she smiled at Silverado, with his glossy gray coat shining, she felt hollow inside. No excitement filled her. Today she'd prove to Chance what kind of trainer she was, prove the validity of her instincts about Silverado. But her victory would be empty.

Chance leaned against the double-hung door to look at his animal. Behind him, Andrea watched racehorses being walked by their grooms. The girl had avoided Liz since her uncle had left, blaming her for another defection. Liz felt pain for Andrea's loss and wanted to comfort her, but couldn't find the words.

"What do you think his chances are today?" Chance asked, casting an oblique glance at her.

"The best." She forced confidence into her voice. Not even Timmy had devastated her this much. She ran a hand through her hair and rubbed eyes that itched from the dust that swirled constantly through the air.

Hundreds of horses waited patiently in the backstretch—some enclosed in their stalls, others being walked. Some would race today, others wouldn't. Horses came and went, huge trailers arriving and departing at the backstretch every day. The winners stayed—horses on their rise to stardom. The losers moved on to other tracks, seeking less rigorous competition.

Liz's whole life revolved around racetracks. Whenever she returned, she felt renewed, as if she'd come home. But this time was different. She couldn't summon the energy. None of the excitement, the anticipation, filled her. She felt dead inside—and alone.

That Winning Touch   149

She ignored the ache in her heart. When Chance turned to her, she knew he saw the same restless hunger in her. And yet the tension between them didn't lessen, but grew. She turned away, seeking control of her runaway emotions. They seemed to have little to say to each other, when before they'd had so much.

"Hey, Liz," a man called. He trotted around a horse, patting the animal, sidestepping a kicking hoof.

The man approached her. Small and delicately built, Mark Fairfax seemed incapable of controlling the huge strength of a thoroughbred caught in the fever of racing. But he had ridden horses for her father, and then for her. She knew he was reliable. She trusted him. He understood horses with a rare combination of empathy and love. Many jockeys rode for money. Mark rode for love.

"Mark Fairfax," Liz said, "this is Chance Brentwood. He owns Silverado and Betsy Ross." She stood aside to let the jockey shake hands with Chance. "Mark is riding Silverado and Betsy Ross today."

"Nice animals you got." Mark patted Silverado, who nuzzled him. Then he smiled at Andrea, who topped him by an inch.

"I'm Andrea." she announced, her eyes looking him up and down curiously.

"Hi, there," Mark responded in a friendly manner. "Liz, the horses look ready. They really have that edge."

She nodded. The last week had been hectic. The track stewards had given permission for the animals to race. She'd entered them in the races they qualified for, deposited the jockey fees with the bookkeeper, and filed the animals' registration papers with the racing secretary. She'd made certain all the licenses were current and legal and all the fees were paid. The blacksmith had left only

150   *That Winning Touch*

an hour ago, having reshoed both horses with lightweight aluminum racing plates. She felt tired and ragged, stretched beyond her ability to cope.

Mark talked to Chance, then said good-bye. Andrea tagged along with him, talking excitedly. He listened with the same patience he used on the horses he rode.

Chance moved closer to Liz, using his cane to negotiate the uneven ground. ''We have to talk.''

She could almost feel his body heat. Her longing for him swept over her. Instead she stepped back, wiping the perspiration beading her temples.

They *did* have to talk. She had made the decision during the last week. She intended to announce her resignation. She was unable to continue working with him.

''After the races,'' she said. A trainer she knew slightly walked by and nodded at her. She returned his politeness with a smile. Women trainers were an oddity. Her father's reputation kept the men on friendly terms with her. Her own reputation gave her acceptance, but her father had paved the way.

''Come to my box to watch the races,'' Chance urged.

''I'll be there.'' She waited awkwardly for him to leave. Her happiness had been so brief. Her grief would live with her the rest of her life.

No more romances would clutter up her life. Timmy had wanted her to destroy her father. Chance didn't trust her. She had cast doubts on Sam's loyalty. How could he choose between a woman he barely knew and a man he'd known all his life?

He left and Liz swallowed her pain.

''Liz!'' The man who approached her had blue eyes with a kindness in their depths that almost brought Liz to tears.

That Winning Touch
151

"Hello, Judd." Warmly, she held out her hands. Judd McLane smiled back, revealing toothless gums. He had dentures, but he seldom wore them, preferring to keep them in his pocket.

"I thought it was you standing there." His voice had a husky, whispery timber to it.

"I thought you retired."

He shook his head. "Not me. I went over to San Luis Rey Downs and got a job as assistant stable manager. The pay ain't so good, but I don't have to travel all over the state no more." He gave a dry chuckle, rubbing a bristled chin as he laughed.

Liz sat down on a bench. Judd followed, sitting down with a sigh, stretching his skinny legs out in front of him and reaching into the breast pocket of his shirt for a cigarette and matches.

"I'm glad to see you," she said. Judd had started out as jockey, but had grown too tall and heavy. Her father offered him a job as assistant trainer. Everything Judd knew about horses he'd learned from her father. Half of what Liz knew, she'd learned from Judd.

"I hear you took over Brentwood's horses," he said. "You shouldn't have taken the job. Sam and that son of his are bad news."

"I heard what happened." Liz knew Judd had never taken kickbacks from suppliers. He had integrity. He lived by the moral ethics instilled in him by her own father.

"I could have killed that Sam Cary. He's no good, Liz. He near ruined my reputation. He'll do the same to you if he can. He's poison." Judd looked around the stable area. Like everyone else involved in racing, he couldn't stay away from the horses. Thoroughbreds were

152   *That Winning Touch*

in his blood. He'd hang around the track till his dying day.

"I'm wise to him." She made no mention of the cut girth on Shay's Pride's saddle or her broken wrist. She wouldn't think about the attack in the Jacuzzi. Absently, she massaged her wrist. The skin was a white band between tanned skin.

"He's got some kind of game goin'," Judd continued. "I don't know what. Be careful, Liz. He's dangerous. Your pa would never forgive me if I let something bad happen to you."

"Tell me what Sam did to you," Liz coaxed. A truck drove by, towing a horse trailer that billowed dust over the roofs of the stables. Inside the trailer, Liz could see the delicate head of a thoroughbred. The trailer stopped at the end of a line of stables. A man got out, walked to the rear, and let down the ramp.

"It was my own darn fault." Judd cracked his knuckles. "I should have known when the accounts didn't balance what Sam was doing. He took the kickbacks, not me."

"Didn't you tell Chance?"

"I tried to, but Sam has him hoodwinked. What would he believe? A story from a man who worked for him for only two months, or someone who'd worked for him all his life? I decided it wasn't worth the argument. I took my pay and left."

Liz told Judd how she'd fired Jack. He chuckled with wry amusement. Finally, he shoved himself to his feet.

"Got to be goin'. Give me a call up at San Luis Rey. I got a nice place on the grounds, nothin' fancy, but at least it's clean. And I know a few owners who'd like you

That Winning Touch   153

to train for them. Got some first-class nags too.'' He chuckled again, waved at Liz, and left her.

She continued to sit on the bench, listening to Silverado's nervous pacing. Allen walked around the corner of the barn and sat down next to her.

''I want to thank you for helping me get my apprentice jockey license,'' he said.

''I'll give your name to a few friends. Maybe they can use you.'' Liz had been glad to sponsor Allen. He had a feel for horses. She thought he'd make a good jockey despite the intense competition among the apprentices. Only a few of them ever went on to become big-money jockeys like Willie Shoemaker.

''I thought maybe you'd let me ride Betsy Ross or Silverado today.'' He stared at her intently.

''I already hired Mark Fairfax.'' Liz smiled to take the sting away from her words. Allen had done a Trojan job training the horses. But she'd needed a name jockey when she entered the horses in their races, and Mark had been available.

Allen frowned. ''But I know them. I know their quirks and what makes them run. You can still make a change if you want.''

''I'm sorry, Allen. With the animals in my charge, I'm just as ruthless as any other trainer. I want the best. You need experience.'' Liz didn't add that jockeys were a dime a dozen.

''How do I get experience when no one will hire me?'' he asked angrily.

''Start asking around. Get to know people. Everyone here started at the bottom. You'll have to do the same.'' Liz stood up. She glanced at her watch, her stomach growling. Post time for the first race was two o'clock.

154 *That Winning Touch*

Silverado was entered in the fifth race, and Betsy Ross in the seventh. Both were allowance races with modest purses of seventeen thousand dollars.

"No favors, then?" he asked, standing with her. He glanced up, his gaze making the long trip.

"I got you your papers," she reminded him gently. What more did he want? "Silverado will still be around when you're ready for him. I'll save a race for you then." She simply had too much at stake to take a chance with Allen.

She glanced at her watch again. She had enough time to get some food, change her clothes, and meet Chance at his box. She wanted a good look at Silverado's first win in six months. He would win today. She could feel it in her blood.

Stretching, she looked up and down the lane. She saw Sam in the picnic area, talking to two heavyset men wearing silk suits already wilted in the heat.

Sam would deliver the horses to the receiving barns in plenty of time before each race. When today ended, he would have the trainer's job he coveted. Chance would give it to him. Having hired and fired four trainers in two years, Chance had earned a reputation he probably didn't deserve, but no one would work for him now.

"I'll see you later, Allen. Don't worry about getting races. You will." She smiled reassuringly at him.

"I don't want to ride strange horses. I want to ride Silverado." His eyes held the hard glitter of anger. His mouth thinned to a slashing line across his face. He glanced at Sam.

"I'm sorry." She did regret his anger, but today was too important to gamble on an inexperienced apprentice.

He stalked away, joining Sam and the strange men.

That Winning Touch 155

Sam looked at her, and she turned away. She had managed to keep the peace between her and Sam until now, and she didn't want to upset the balance of her self-control.

At the showers, Liz washed and changed from work jeans to a blue silk floral dress and low-heeled sandals. After tossing her duffel bag in the back of her Mazda, she headed toward the grandstand early enough to get lunch before joining Chance. They'd watch the races, then talk, and Chance would find out she wouldn't be working for him anymore. She'd miss his horses, but she'd have others. Maybe she'd even move a little closer to her dream of having her own training facility and breeding service.

Chance sat in his box, nodding at friends and acquaintances, wondering where Liz was. A waiter took his order for iced tea.

He tried to enjoy the beauty around him. Del Mar was one of the prettiest tracks in California, but he found he couldn't relax. The days spent away from Liz had been horrible: troubled nights tossing and turning, unable to sleep. But it gave him time to examine what had happened between them. His conclusion? The whole situation had been his fault.

One morning while he watched the sun rise over the balustrade of his apartment patio, he had made a decision: He would retire Sam; he had outlived his usefulness. Sam turned sixty on his next birthday, old enough to enjoy the life of leisure and the pension promised him. Chance didn't want to know if Sam had been cheating him.

While he had struggled with his decision, he'd recognized his unfairness to Liz. He had hired her to train

156 *That Winning Touch*

a winner. She had done just that. He had wronged her and the other trainers who had worked for him, summarily dismissing them even when they had shown him evidence of fraud. He had never questioned Sam's statements.

Chance knew he could find out about Sam. He had hired detectives for other cases; he could hire one to investigate Sam. But he didn't. Sam was a part of his family, a friend and mentor. Whatever he'd done, Chance didn't want to know.

"Uncle Chance?" Andrea tossed a sweater on the chair. Blond hair fell loose about her face. "I'm going to find Liz."

Here was another problem Chance had to deal with. Andrea's anger at him had flared into a shouting match in the car on the way to the track. He had been as unfair to her as he'd been to Liz. How would he make it up to her? He loved her. She meant more to him than anyone in the world.

"Okay," he answered, watching her go. She bobbed through the crowd, darting around people and running down the ramp.

The clubhouse seats were mostly full. He could see streams of people moving around the grandstands. A thrill of excitement electrified him. He loved racing, a love inherited from his father. Though he seldom bet on the horses, he still enjoyed picking winners. Today would be his day to have his own winner.

He never doubted that Silverado would make a spectacular win. Liz had been so confident about the horse. Chance had caught her excitement and confidence.

"Excuse me. Mr. Brentwood?"

Chance looked up at a tall, elderly man with pure white

That Winning Touch   157

hair, natty mustache, and smiling blue eyes. He wore a blue sports coat and a white shirt over white trousers.

"I'm Charles Gingham. Can you come with me, please?"

"Is something wrong?" Chance grabbed his cane and rose to his feet. He swallowed the last of his iced tea and followed the man into the aisle, stumbling when his cane caught in the pole divider separating his box from the next.

"Only a small problem." Gingham refused to answer any more questions. Chance followed him, trying not to let worry overcome his good sense.

Liz ate a hurried lunch in the restaurant. She walked into the area reserved for people with private boxes and hurried up the ramp and down the aisle. The box was empty. Where was Chance? The remains of a glass of iced tea testified that he'd been here.

She scanned the crowd, hoping to see him talking with a friend. Instead she saw a woman who from the back looked a lot like Dicey Anderson. She was talking to a man Liz thought she recognized, but no name came to her.

She opened the racing program, going over the entries in each race. She recognized most of the names. She waved at people she knew.

"Hello, darling," Dicey purred.

Liz twisted around. Dicey stood in the aisle, two blond surfer types clinging to her sides. She wore a scanty halter top and shorts, a golf cap tilted jauntily.

Liz stared. "Where's Paul?"

A surge of pain swept across Dicey's face. "In Europe.'' She gazed up at the young men, a hard-edged glimmer in her eyes. ''We had . . . a fight.''

Liz had thought Dicey was finally in love, but now she had reverted to her old self—the person Liz detested. They had come so close to understanding each other.

Dicey shook off the two young men with shooing gestures and pointed at an empty box on the next level. Then she leaned over the divider pole with a conspiratorial wink. ''I saw Chance in Los Angeles,'' she said in a dramatic whisper. ''He had the most gorgeous starlet on his arm. You've seen her on television doing those perfume commercials for—''

''Stop, Dicey. This isn't you.'' Liz didn't want to hear. A knife seemed to go through her, cutting her heart in half. The pain brought tears to her eyes.

''What do you mean?'' Suddenly, Dicey looked like a little girl who'd lost herself.

''Get rid of those bums and find Paul.'' At least one person should be happy. Dicey deserved better.

''I have my pride.'' She drew herself up stiffly.

''So?'' Liz replied.

Dicey drew back. ''Chance isn't happy. Did you two have a fight? Are you still working for him?''

''I'm considering quitting.''

Dicey patted her arm. ''Tell me all about it.''

''Maybe later.'' Liz turned away. She wouldn't share her grief with Dicey. ''Go find Paul. You two are so right for each other.''

''I'm sorry. You don't seem to have much luck in love.'' Dicey's voice sounded sincerely concerned.

Liz smiled. ''Neither do you. But you can change that. Don't throw away your chances.'' Liz fidgeted. The clock on the betting board showed twenty minutes to the first

That Winning Touch   159

race. The horses would be filing into the paddock area to be saddled.

"Don't throw away yours."

When Liz looked back, Dicey was gone. She refused to look in the direction of Dicey's private box. She didn't want to see her fawning over those two muscle-bound men.

The loudspeaker came on with a screech that hurt people's ears. "Will Liz Stratton please report to the racing office. Will Liz Stratton report to the racing office."

Puzzled, Liz glanced around. Dicey had half-risen in her seat, but she ignored her.

"What's the problem?" Liz asked when she entered the racing office, a neutral room with functional furniture overflowing with magazines, newspapers, and racing charts.

Chance looked pained and angry, accusations on his face. Charles Gingham, one of the track stewards, approached her.

"Hello, Liz," Gingham said cordially, though a hint of steel lingered in his tone.

"You'd better sit down," Chance said.

Liz remained standing, facing the steward, staring at him. An awful, horrible fear attacked her.

"I'm sorry," Gingham said softly, "but your horses have been scratched."

Liz stared at him, disbelieving. She shook her head to clear it. "Why?" She strangled on the word.

Gingham held up a sheet of paper. "Lab report." He handed it to her. "We took urine samples this morning. We found very high levels of butazolidin in both your animals. I'm sorry to have to say this, but you're also restricted from the track pending an investigation."

Liz stumbled. Her mind seemed stuck. She grabbed the back of a chair, her legs no longer capable of holding her. Chance reached out for her, but she pushed him away and sat down.

"Are you taking my license?"

Gingham shook his head. "Not until we get the facts. But we can't permit any entries from your stable until all your horses have been tested. I am truly sorry. I find this terribly hard to believe. I've known you since you were a child. I'm certain there is a logical explanation for this."

Liz covered her face with her hands. In the back of her mind, she knew Sam had wounded her in the best way possible. He was behind this. Or was he?

After six weeks in his company, she suddenly began to wonder if Sam had the intelligence to dream up something like this. Her experience with him said no. This possible destruction of her career had a more vindictive feel to it than Sam seemed capable of.

She stood up. "I'm sorry too, Mr. Gingham. You must believe me. I have given no illegal drugs of any kind to any of my animals. What made you test them?" Urine tests were usually done after the race.

Gingham looked uncomfortable. "An anonymous phone call."

He said to Chance, "Until your animals are certified free of drugs by the track vet and an independent vet, they can't race anywhere in this state. I'm sorry, Mr. Brentwood."

"So am I." Chance sounded grim and angry.

He took Liz's hand and held on even when she tried to shake him away. He hung on until they stood outside the racing office staring at each other.

"Let go of me!" she growled.

That Winning Touch   161

"No."

He held on as they walked up the ramp and entered the box just as the race announcer started to call the scratches for the day. Silverado and Betsy Ross headed the list. Liz flinched at the sound of their names, feeling as if she would burst into tears again.

"What a shame!" Dicey cried in sympathy as she entered the box. She reached out, and Liz found her embrace unusually comforting. She leaned her head against Dicey's shoulder, hot tears filling her eyes. "Can I help?"

"Thanks, Dicey, but not at the moment," Chance said roughly. He looked around. "Where's Andrea?"

"I haven't seen her," Liz said.

He picked up Andrea's sweater. "She went to find you."

Liz shook her head. "After you left, I showered, had lunch, and came here. I never saw her."

"Let's find her. Then we're going to figure out what happened with Silverado and Betsy Ross."

"Let me help," Dicey said. "I'll check the stands."

"Sam Cary . . ." Liz responded bitterly.

"Listen, I've known Sam all my life. He's never once done something like this. He's done a lot of little things, petty things, but nothing like this."

"You don't know that."

"I don't believe Sam is responsible." Chance shook his head, eyes skeptical.

In a way, neither did Liz. And yet, the evidence pointed at Sam. He had been taking kickbacks from suppliers. He had access to the blacksmith who did the shoeing. And he had a reason.

"I can't bother about Sam now. We have to find Andrea and get this mess straightened out.'' Chance took Andrea's sweater. Then he turned and walked away, dragging Liz along with him, refusing to let go of her hand even when she protested.

Chapter Ten

"What's butazolidin?" Chance asked as they walked past the paddock and into the receiving area.

They dodged horses, grooms, and jockeys. A dog strained against a leash. A goat on a similar lead munched happily on a weed. A horse neighed, followed by the crow of a rooster.

"It's an analgesic." Liz hurried to keep up with Chance. When he wanted to move, he managed efficiently despite his bad leg. "It keeps a horse from feeling pain by blocking the pain."

They turned down the lane leading to the backstretch. On their right the pony barns looked hazy in the dust that rose with each blast of ocean breeze. Beyond was the parking lot, where hundreds of people still hurried along the gravel lanes into the track to get in before post time.

Horses for the next race passed them. Liz tried not to think about Silverado and Betsy Ross. All her work for nothing. Tonight she'd be out of a job, most likely out of a career. What would she do now? She tried not to think about her problem, but her thoughts whirled around in her head until a headache started, first at the base of her neck and then behind her eyes.

163

164 *That Winning Touch*

Chance stopped a man to ask about Andrea. The man shook his head and walked on.

Liz saw Judd. She waved at him. "Have you seen Andrea Brentwood?" How could one young girl get lost so easily?

"She was with Mark Fairfax a little while ago," Judd replied. He led a tall, rangy-legged sorrel mare who tossed her head and rolled her brown eyes. When she sidestepped nervously, he reached out to scratch her sensitive lip. The mare quieted, but the whites of her eyes still showed.

"Where's Mark now?" The lines in Chance's face deepened with worry. He looked sharply about, hoping to spot Andrea walking among the horses and their handlers, now heading toward the receiving barn.

"Getting ready to ride. He's got a mount in the first race." Judd tugged the mare onward. Her tail swished nervously.

Infected with Chance's rising worry, Liz said, "Mark's saddling up now. We'll have to wait till after the race. We can catch him in the barns before his next race."

"Let's check the backstretch. Maybe she's with Sam." Chance held on to Liz. She matched his stride, understanding what drove him. The same worry drove her. Her hand seemed to fit into his naturally, reminding her of the day at the fair.

A blond-maned pony with a broken rein darted past them, the rider following on foot. Liz grabbed the trailing rein and stopped the pony with a sharp jerk. The animal stood still, skin rippling spasmodically over its withers.

"Thanks," the rider said, his posting jacket dusty from his fall. "Ginger's excited today." He led the pony away.

That Winning Touch 165

Liz trotted to catch up with Chance. "Andrea's all right. There's no reason to think otherwise."

Chance asked each person who passed them, describing Andrea. Sweat plastered his hair to his forehead. His eyes looked shadowed and faded.

"She said she'd find you and walk back to the grandstand with you. Andrea always does what she says." Chance watched a young girl a few years older than Andrea. The girl led a chestnut mare, her small hands clamped on the reins, her round face grimy with dust and sweat.

Liz walked through the gate and into the backstretch. The barns were a hive of activity. Two pickup trucks, parked in front of the feed store, held sacks of grain and bales of straw. A Labrador retriever, sitting on top of a bale, stared at Liz and Chance. A calico barn cat stalked mice among the bags of grain.

Sam was gone; the table he'd sat at empty. Liz saw nothing of Allen.

"Liz?" A groom stopped her—a thin, wiry man about twenty years old with muscular arms and bowed legs, dressed in worn jeans and patched vest. He wore a baseball cap turned sideways. "I heard your horses were scratched. I'm sorry to hear about you being restricted. If it's any consolation, I don't believe you'd do something like that—riskin' your reputation and all."

Liz stiffened. The grapevine, already at work, had broadcast the news of her disgrace. "Thanks, Hank. We'll get it all straightened out." She spoke more confidently than she felt.

"I don't know if this would help, but that groom you brought along from your farm has been saying some pretty

166 *That Winning Touch*

nasty things about you.'' Hank looked nervously at his scuffed shoes.

''I'm sure he has.'' The wry tone in her voice startled her. Sam hadn't had anything good to say about her since her arrival. His rancor had increased with the blossoming of her love for Chance. She had managed this last week through sheer guts and determination, mixed with a heaping tablespoon of diplomacy she didn't think herself capable of.

Chance stopped and turned back to Hank. ''What kind of things?'' He grabbed Hank's arm.

''Sorry, sir.'' Hank smiled, politely unwilling to divulge anything. The grooms and handlers were a tight-knit group. They seldom talked to anyone not directly a part of the racing crowd.

''Hank,'' Liz interrupted, ''this is Chance Brentwood. He owns the scratched horses.'' She worried about what Hank would say.

The groom looked interested. He chewed gum, rolling the wad back and forth in his mouth. ''Well. . . . This fellow, Sam, who came with Liz, has a pretty mean mouth. Told me and a buddy that he would get even with her for firing his son. I'm afraid we didn't listen much. A lot of people around here complain. You got to let them have their airtime and then forget it.''

''What else?'' Chance persisted.

Hank chewed his gum for a moment. ''Sam seems to think Liz caused him a powerful lot of trouble. He had somethin' in his mind. Didn't say what, though.''

Chance let Hank go. The groom pushed his baseball cap back on his head, and stringy brown strands of hair fell forward.

''I'm sorry, Chance.'' Liz touched him.

That Winning Touch   167

"Mr. Brentwood," Hank continued, "if I were you, I'd get rid of that man. He's got poison in him. That ain't good for the horses." He shrugged, then continued on his way.

"All this time," Chance said, "I trusted Sam."

"Sam doesn't intend to hurt you. Even I know how much he loves you." Troubled by the quiet intensity of his anger, Liz began to throb with her own pain over his hurt.

"Maybe not, but he's hurt people I love. Not even Sam has that right. I should have listened to Andrea. She tried to tell me." Chance's voice sounded angry and regretful. His suffering showed in his face. Liz forgot her anger, her love returning, growing into something stronger, more durable.

"Andrea's fine," Liz said. "I know she is." They turned down the block of stables that housed Silverado.

Sam sat on the bench at the end of a row of box stalls. He looked lost and old, with his mouth sagging open and his eyes unfocused yet wary.

"Sam!" Chance called.

He hitched himself to his feet like a disjointed puppet. Puffs of dust rose from his clothes. He pulled his straw hat from his head, ran a hand through his hair, and reseated the hat.

"Have you seen Andrea?" Chance demanded.

Sam stared at the road leading away from the fairgrounds to the highway and the freeway beyond. Then he shrugged. Liz sensed his fear.

"She's with Allen," Sam said finally, his voice tired. He looked at Chance for the first time, then looked quickly away.

"Did he take her home?" Chance asked.

168 *That Winning Touch*

"No." Sam turned haunted eyes, pinched with pain, on Liz. He spoke directly to her, avoiding Chance. "I tried to stop him, but Allen wouldn't listen. He said if he left Andrea here, you'd have the police after him."

"I'll call security," Liz said, turning back toward the feed store where she knew she'd find a phone. "You start searching the barn area, Chance. He can't have gotten far." The Klaxon sound of a bell announced the twenty-minute time limit for the next race. Time to get the next field of horses to the paddock. She glanced at her watch. It was after two-thirty. The first and second race had been run. She wondered who'd won. Then she entered the feed store and dialed the racing office.

It was when Liz was on her way back to join Chance and Sam that she spotted Allen near the feed store. He was alone, and she hurried after him, hoping he'd lead her to Andrea. She thought he was unaware of her presence, but when she darted after him into a narrow passageway, she discovered she was wrong. He was waiting on a high ledge, a rock in his hand. Before she could run, he had leaped upon her and knocked her to the ground. Then everything went black. . . .

"Tell me about what's going on, Sam." Chance sat down on the bench next to the old man after Liz left. For the first time, he really saw Sam for what he was—old, tired, and used-up. He felt no real animosity toward him. The man had his dreams.

"Allen thought up the idea." Sam's voice began without inflection. He looked down at his hands. "He told me what to do. He said it would be easy because you'd make me head trainer." He stopped talking, took a

That Winning Touch 169

breath, and pushed gray hair off his forehead. He lit a cigarette.

"What idea?"

"Allen had the contacts. . . ."

Chance felt his heart go cold. "Contacts?"

"To sell the stuff."

"What stuff, Sam?" Chance tried to coax him into faster revelations, but he wouldn't be hurried.

"Cocaine, of course. There's a lot of money in drugs." His voice grew hollow as he stared at the track.

"How?" *Hurry up, Andrea's life is at stake*, he thought.

"The dealers knew when we had to move the stuff. Silverado, or any of the other horses, would come in dead last. That was the signal to contact me and I'd arrange to transfer the stuff.

"Allen said we'd make a lot of money. But you kept hiring new trainers we had to get rid of. Then you hired Liz. She's nobody's fool. Even Allen saw we couldn't get rid of her the same way as the others." Sam slumped against the barn.

Chance felt sick. He thought he knew Sam. How could he have misjudged these people so easily? He'd known Allen Jaffe since his family moved to Del Mar and Allen came looking for work when he was fourteen.

"Allen is the one who cut the girth on Shay's Pride. I'm sorry Liz broke her wrist." Sam puffed on his cigarette.

"Go on, Sam." Chance glanced around. Liz had not yet returned. Where was she?

"He's the one who tried to drown Liz. I didn't know nothin' until later. We argued. Allen said he just wanted to frighten her. But Liz didn't frighten. She got mad."

170　　　　*That Winning Touch*

"Why did you go along with it, Sam?"

"Needed the money. Jack's been gambling a bit. He hits the card parlors in University City on weekends. When the racing season starts, he bets the horses." Sam continued, his voice slowing as he searched for the words. "He had these special shoes made for the horses. The shoes caused their stride to be off." Sam stubbed his cigarette out against the planking of the bench.

A security car turned the corner and stopped. Charles Gingham got out, followed by two armed guards.

Sam fiddled with the cuff of his sleeve. "Allen is the one who told me to rub the liniment containing the butazolidin on the horses. Liz would be blamed. Then I'd be head trainer.

"Andrea heard us," he went on, his voice taking on a flat, grim tone. "We were talking, sitting on this bench and she was inside with Silverado. I thought she'd gone to watch the first race, but she come bustin' out yelling. She's a tiger, that one, sticking up for you." Sam shook his head in wonderment, then lapsed into a morose stare. "Wish my Jack was more like her."

Gingham cleared his throat. "We'll have to get statements on this. I think this will clear Liz of all charges, but, unfortunately, until a formal hearing, the current status stands. By the way, where is she?"

"I don't know. She never came back from the feed store." Chance had started to worry. He turned to Sam and said softly, "Where is Andrea?"

Sam glanced at the security officers casting long shadows on the ground. "Allen said not to look for her. You should go home and he'd call and tell you where she is. He promised not to hurt her."

Chance could only think about how frightened Andrea

That Winning Touch   171

probably was. How would he get her back now? He tried
to concentrate on what Sam had said, but a deep, growing
anger prevented him.

Gingham took charge. He ordered one guard to put
Sam in the car and to call the police. He held a modular
phone in one hand. He dialed the gate and learned Allen
had not yet signed out of the track. Gingham ordered
Allen to be taken into custody. Then he asked for rein-
forcements and started searching the barn area.

"He'll be stopped at the gate, Mr. Brentwood,"
Gingham said, "and the police will be here in a few
minutes. Do you have a picture of your niece? What is
she wearing?"

Chance dug out his wallet and flipped it open to Andrea's last school picture. He handed the picture to
Gingham, who gave it to the security officer.

Anguish overwhelmed Chance. He couldn't remember
what Andrea wore. Where was Liz? He cleared his throat.
A picture of Andrea appeared in his mind. "Andrea's
wearing blue shorts and a white T-shirt with Minnie
Mouse silk-screened on the front and a Disneyland logo
on the back. Her hair's a little longer than in this picture.
She's about five feet tall and wearing pink sneakers—the
high-top kind the kids wear these days."

The post bell for the third race sounded, filtering over
the backstretch. After a few minutes, the thunder of racing
hooves sounded, then all was silence again. A flock of
sea gulls swooped down on the picnic area fighting for
scraps.

"We'll get your niece back," Gingham said. More
security cars zoomed toward them.

"Liz appears to be missing now too."

"We'll find them both." Gingham turned toward the

172 *That Winning Touch*

security guards and rapidly explained everything. Chance listened, nodding in the right places and answering questions tossed at him. He gave a description of Allen. Everyone already knew Liz. He talked to each guard while Gingham showed Andrea's picture. When the security force dispersed, Chance started searching on his own.

Liz woke with the smell of damp straw in her nostrils and a dull ache in the back of her head. She tried to think where she was, but couldn't remember. She opened her eyes. The box stall was shadowed with shafts of light showing through the cracks in the timbered walls. A horse moved nervously about and Liz heard the sound of someone crying.

She rolled over. "Who's there?" She could just make out a small figure lying on the straw a few feet away.

"Liz?" Andrea said, her voice heavy with relief. "I thought you were dead."

"Well, I'm not." Liz tried to touch her head, but discovered her hands were bound behind her. "Are you all right?"

Andrea sniffled. "I think so."

"Can you move?"

"No. Allen tied me up." Straw rustled under her.

Allen, Liz thought, and remembered how he'd ambushed her. She pulled experimentally at the ropes binding her. The knots were tight. She could barely move her fingers. "Do you know where we are?"

"Silverado's stall."

"Good. Someone will find us soon." Liz could feel Silverado moving more nervously now. She listened to the thud of his hooves on the concrete floor beneath the straw.

That Winning Touch   173

"I hope so," Andrea sobbed. "I'm afraid."

Liz tried to move, scooting across the straw toward Andrea. She made slow progress, taking minutes to cover a foot. "I'm here," she soothed. "We'll be all right."

As soon as the words left her mouth, she knew she'd spoken too soon. Silverado snorted. A wisp of smoke snaked along the floor of the box stall and into Liz's nose. She rolled toward Andrea, conscious of her wrist starting to hurt again, the break not yet healed, the muscles straining beneath the ropes.

She had to get to Andrea. If they kept their heads, she might be able to untie Andrea. The smoke grew thicker. Silverado paced back and forth in front of the door, tossing his head. He gave a mighty trumpeting sound and kicked the wall.

Liz bumped into Andrea. "See if you can untie me."

"I can't. My hands are numb. Are we going to die? Do I smell smoke? Someone set fire to the barn!"

Liz heard the distinct crackle of fire. She caught a glimpse of an orange finger of flame moving up the back wall of the stall. Silverado kicked the wall again. Allen was a lot smarter than she'd thought. If Silverado didn't kill them with his panicked stamping, then the fire would.

A hoof grazed Liz's shoulder. She recoiled from the pain. Andrea started to scream. Liz tried to reach the ropes on Andrea's wrists, but her fingers refused to cooperate. The fire grew larger. Silverado became more panicked. Another stamping hoof grazed Liz's ribs. She gasped in pain, her vision going black. Spots floated in front of her eyes. She moved as close to Andrea as she could, the thought of protecting her hazily filling her mind.

174 *That Winning Touch*

The door crashed open. A shape outlined against the blue sky was followed by a second figure, then a third.

"Uncle Chance?" Andrea screamed.

Silverado darted out of the stall. Chance grabbed Liz, and Gingham grabbed Andrea and pulled her to safety.

Liz gagged with the smoke. A fireman rushed into the stall with a hose. Liz saw enough of the barn area to know that the fire would be under control quickly. The box stalls on either side of Silverado were quickly being emptied. The horses were saved. Then she plunged into darkness.

"This is getting to be a habit," Liz said as she lay on the examining table in the track infirmary in a fetal position, trying to ignore the pain in her side. A gray-haired doctor fussed over her. Andrea lay on a second table, her face pinched and wan. Chance held her hand and looked at Liz.

"I'm just thankful you're alive." He smiled at her.

She allowed a nurse to coax her into straightening her legs. She was conscious of a dozen different aches and pains and bruises and worried that she might have a couple of broken ribs. X rays had been taken earlier and the doctor was waiting for the results while he bandaged Andrea's scrapes and cuts.

A uniformed police officer entered and introduced himself as Sargeant Anderson of the Del Mar Police Department.

"We have Allen Jaffe and Sam Cary in custody," he announced. "You'll have to come down to the station and sign your statements, Mr. Brentwood."

"I'll be there as soon as I get my niece and Miss Stratton home and into bed," Chance told him.

That Winning Touch 175

Liz felt limp and lethargic. So much had happened in the last few hours. She only wanted the day to end so she could go home and sleep.

"Jaffe tried to sneak out the gate during the fire. Security took him into custody," Anderson said.

Chance nodded. He looked haggard and haunted. He stretched his leg out in front of him, resting it on a stool.

The last hours had been ones Liz never wanted to repeat. A technician entered the room and handed the doctor two X rays. He placed them on a screen and turned the light on.

"Well, Miss Stratton," the doctor said, "you've got a couple of broken ribs and a badly sprained shoulder, but there's no permanent damage. I'll just tape those ribs and see to the little girl and send you both home for some rest."

When darkness covered the barns, Liz let herself out of her apartment and walked toward the pool. The doctor had given her something to make her sleep, but now, at midnight, she was wide-awake. Her ribs hurt and her shoulder ached, but she felt happy to be alive.

"Want to sit in the Jacuzzi for a few minutes?" Chance asked. He was sitting on a chaise near the pool, waiting for her.

"All right. I suppose I can dangle my legs in the water." They walked over to the Jacuzzi. He flipped on the motor and she sat on the side, her legs resting in the swirling hot water.

"Last time we did this, we were in love with each other." A dry tone crept into Liz's voice. She blushed uneasily.

"I'm still in love with you."

She swiveled around to look at him. He smiled. The tension in his face released.

He leaned back in the water, spreading his arms across the lip of the Jacuzzi. "This feels good. I've been doing a lot of thinking." He ran a finger down the length of her leg. "I almost allowed the best people in my life to get away."

Liz shivered despite the rising steam and warmth of the water. She rested a hand against his shoulder. In one easy movement, he rose out of the water and put his arms gently around her and drew her close.

"I'm not letting you get away, Liz Stratton. As for Andrea, life is going to be different around here. I've decided to open an office here in Rancho Santa Fe and just take a few jobs here and there. Nothing time consuming or too big to handle. I'm going to turn my L.A. office over to my partners. And I'm going to start enjoying life with the people who mean the most to me. No more long-distance parenting for Andrea. She's going to find out what it's like to have a twenty-four-hour uncle and father. Furthermore, I want to marry you. Will you marry me, Liz?" he whispered in her ear.

She jerked away to stare at him. "I. . . ."

"You don't have to answer now."

She could see he was disappointed. She reached out to stroke his chest. "Yes, I'll marry you."

She didn't want to think about the difficulties yet. She didn't want to think about juggling a career and a marriage. She sank into the circle of his arms, raising her lips to his. He felt so good close to her, in her arms. She couldn't let him go. Not now. Not ever.

Chapter Eleven

SILVERADO pranced, tail held high, mane flowing in the wind, ears alert. Mark Fairfax clung to the horse, wearing purple and gray silks, the sleeves fluttering.

Liz stood at the rail, watching as the horses went into the gate. Behind her the restless mood of the crowd washed over the track. Wind rippled the water of the pond.

Chance slid an arm around her. Behind them in the private seating, Andrea stood on her chair, binoculars in her hands. Pete tugged at her, yelling, his words carried away by the wind.

"This is it," Liz said to Chance. He smiled down at her. She held her own binoculars and trained them on the gate.

The bell rang, the gates snapped open, and the horses raced out onto the track, dirt flying.

"Silverado's primed today," Chance said.

The crowd yelled, stamped, and screamed. Around them, the people in the reserved clubhouse seating rushed to the rail, pushing at those already there.

The horses flew around the first turn. Silverado looked boxed between two other horses, crowding the inside rail.

177

178   *That Winning Touch*

The track announcer's voice blared over the loudspeaker, giving the details. Silverado was in fifth place.

Liz shrugged off the woman crowding next to her. She trained her glasses on the horses, bunched together now. It was hard to see the positions.

The second turn. The horses whipped past the third furlong pole, the race half over. Liz's heart flip flopped with excitement. She breathed quickly.

The field of racers pounded down the backstretch. Liz saw a blur of silver suddenly break free of the field.

"Too soon," she whispered. With binoculars trained on the horse and rider, she saw that Silverado was in charge, not Mark. Silverado wanted this win to make up for all the ones he'd lost.

The field pounded into the homestretch. The crowd screamed. Chance gripped Liz's arm so tightly, the circulation felt cut off.

Silverado gleamed like a silver strand as he moved ahead of the field and left it behind. He flashed under the wire a full eight lengths ahead of the rest of the horses.

"We did it!" Liz screamed. "We did it!"

Chance kissed her. She clung to him. The crowd seemed to drop away as they faced each other. The warm glow of love filled her, overflowed into him. For a moment, they stood alone among the ten thousand people who surrounded them.

"Uncle Chance!" Andrea rushed up to them, elbowing people out of her way. "Silverado won! He really did win." She glanced down at the betting ticket Chance had bought for her. "And I won fifty dollars!" Silverado was a long shot for the last time in his career.

"As soon as the win is finalized, I'll collect your winnings," Chance told Andrea.

That Winning Touch 179

Liz fingered her own ticket in her pocket. Her own confidence in Silverado had not overcome her natural caution. Her two-dollar ticket brought her twenty dollars. She smiled, knowing Chance had bet much more—not just money, but trust.

He smiled at her. His tanned face bent over hers and he kissed her, on the forehead, then on the lips. She threw her arms around him, the engagement ring on her finger flashing in the hot August sunlight. A modest emerald flanked by two sapphires and two diamonds winked at her. In two weeks a wedding ring would be added, a circlet of emeralds, sapphires, and diamonds. She felt lucky.

"Let's go to the Winner's Circle," she said.

Silverado pranced about the corner of the paddock that served as the Winner's Circle. A photographer faced him. Mark sat in the saddle, relaxed and grinning.

"Great race, Mark," Liz complimented him.

He smiled proudly. "This horse never gave me a chance. He just took the bit and never let go till the finish line." Mark grinned again for the photographer.

Someone handed Liz a bouquet of flowers. She turned briefly toward the camera, then handed the flowers to Andrea and shoved her in front of her uncle. She stepped out of the picture and let the two of them be the center of attention.

Silverado was led away. Mark would dismount in a minute to weigh in, then get ready for his next race.

"That's it," Chance said wryly. "One moment of glory."

"Just wait for the payback." Liz looked down at her ring. She began to understand her own need for payback.

180   *That Winning Touch*

Not in the glory of the win but in the beauty of Chance's love.

She'd reluctantly given up her future with racing, settling for being a wife. She'd worried about the loss of her thoroughbreds and the loss of her identity. She recognized she couldn't do both. Racing took too much time, too much traveling, to make a marriage work. Though racing was a part of her, she felt the time had come to change.

"Let's go home," Chance said.

Silverado was the only entry for the day from Brentwood Farms. Liz had no need to stay. "Let me check Silverado first," she said. "I'll meet you at the car."

Chance nodded. He took Andrea's hand and threaded their way through the crowd gathering at the paddock to watch the saddle-up for the next race. Pete followed with a backward look at Liz. She grinned at him. He waved.

Liz moved into the receiving area. She found the groom in charge of Silverado and spoke with him briefly. Carefully, she checked for any weakness in his legs, or bruises, cuts, and scrapes.

"He's in fine fettle," the groom said.

"See that he's pampered a little for the rest of the day. A nice long walk and a good rubdown."

"Stop worrying. Judd McLane knows his business. He'll see that I treat this fellow properly."

The hardest part of leaving racing was giving up the horses. Liz had turned over Chance's animals to Judd McLane, who had discovered that the quiet life didn't suit him. She saw him as she walked back toward the paddock. He nodded at her.

"Great race," he said over his shoulder.

Liz ran out, trying to keep the lump in her throat down

That Winning Touch   181

to manageable proportions. She walked quickly toward the reserved-parking area where Chance waited for his car. Just as she walked up to him, the Mercedes arrived. The valet opened all the doors. Liz got in and he closed it with a thud.

Chance followed back roads, staying away from the main highways clogged with traffic. Liz tilted her head against the headrest. Absently, she twisted the ring on her finger as she listened to Andrea and Pete still talking excitedly about Silverado's spectacular win.

Suddenly, she felt Chance's hand on hers. She opened her eyes to look at him. He took a folded envelope from his pocket and gave it to her.

"What's this?" she asked curiously.

"Open it. I wanted to give it to you earlier, but decided to wait." Merriment danced in his eyes.

She hesitated, staring at the envelope. Events moved so quickly in the last two weeks. She'd been cleared of all charges and reinstated as a trainer. Sam and Allen were awaiting trial. And Chance and Andrea had moved toward a resolution of their own problems.

"Go on, open it," Chance coaxed. "Nothing inside bites."

Liz tore open the envelope and took out a piece of paper. She opened it, smoothing it across her lap.

"I don't understand." She sat bolt upright as she read.

"It's a line of credit." He grinned like a boy opening presents at Christmas. "I had to liquidate some assets before I could get it for you. It's all yours."

"What am I going to do with this?"

Chance laughed, his voice resounding loudly about the car. Andrea and Pete fell silent. "I know how much racing means to you. Since you're giving up what you love most, I thought I should help you find something else to do. I think Brentwood Farms would make a perfect breeding farm. There's enough money to keep you going for four or five years while you build your stock and get the breeding program started."

Liz stared at the piece of paper. Her future stared back at her. She thought of Silverado and the winners he'd sire. She thought of Betsy Ross, too old for racing but showing herself to be a steady winner. What a mother she'd be.

"I don't know what to say." Touched by his concern, words failed her.

"Thank you is all I need." He glanced at her as he halted at a Stop sign. A little farther on, he turned into the drive leading to Pete's house.

"Thank you." Liz found herself grinning widely. "I'd do more, but this isn't the place."

Chance stopped the car. He waved merrily at Pete's mother. He turned to Liz and winked. "I can't wait."

Liz threw her arms about his neck and kissed him loudly on the lips.

"Wow!" Andrea said.

"Wow!" Chance added.

Pete slammed the door and ran across the drive. Chance put the car in gear, turned around, and headed toward home. Liz sighed, never believing that she could be so wonderfully joyous. She clutched the letter in her hands, feeling the love that went into it, the love he showered on her.

"Wow!" she whispered and turned to smile broadly at the man who had brought her true happiness.